To Love

Nate

A companion to Aaron's Anguish

J.L.Dawson

To Love Nate

By J L Dawson

Butterfly Books
PUBLISHING

Cover design and editing by: Amber Smith
amber.smith40005@gmail.com

ISBN (Paperback) 978-1-7385962-4-9
ISBN (E-book) 978-1-7385962-5-6

A CiP catalogue record for this title is available from the National Library of New Zealand.

First edition, 2023 Butterfly Books Publishing

Contact the author or subscribe to newsletter:
jldawsonauthor@yahoo.com
www.jodawsonauthor.com

Contents

Chapter One	1
Chapter Two	10
Chapter Three	18
Chapter Four	26
Chapter Five	33
Chapter Six	48
Chapter Seven	57
Chapter Eight	68
Chapter Nine	86
Chapter Ten	96
Chapter Eleven	103
Chapter Twelve	116
Chapter Thirteen	127
Chapter Fourteen	136
Chapter Fifteen	150
Chapter Sixteen	165
Epilogue	172
About the Author	178
Other Books by J.L.Dawson	179

One

Bess Carter knelt at her friend's feet with a mouth full of pins, tucking up the hem of the new lavender gown, at ankle height.

"I can't believe we're graduating tomorrow." Amber clasped her hands together and shrugged.

"Ffftand fftill," Bess muttered around the pins, looking up at her friend. She grimaced as the hem pulled out of her hand again.

"Sorry." Amber dropped her arms and stood still before the mirror.

Bess hurried to finish the job before the restless girl began moving again. She slipped the last pin from her mouth and deftly wove it into the fabric. "Almost done." She stretched the hem in her hands, checking by eye that the line was straight. Standing up, she looked at her friend in the long mirror. "I think that's good; now, change out of the gown and I'll get to hemming it."

Amber smiled and turned so Bess could help her with the buttons. "I'm grateful for you helping me with my dress."

"It's my pleasure. You know I love sewing." Bess finished the last button and opened and closed her damaged hand a few times, stretching the sore muscles.

Amber grimaced as she lifted the gown over her head. "Your hand hurting you?"

Bess flashed her a smile, took the gown from her friend, and sat on the bed. "It's just a bit sore when I do lots of finicky work. I finished the beading on my gown

1

before I came to you and it's aching a bit." She shrugged and sucked on the end of her thread. Holding up the needle, she closed one eye and poked the purple thread through the hole.

Amber thrust her brown house dress over her head and shimmied it down over her body. "You don't have to do it now; it can wait till later."

"I need to get it done now. I still have to get supper on for Aaron."

Amber rolled her eyes. "Your brother can make his own supper."

"I don't mind. He works so hard, and he's allowed me to stay at school all these years when I could've been working to help make ends meet. The least I can do is look after him."

"I'm not sure why. He's so mean." Amber finished the last button and plonked herself down on the bed next to Bess, dislodging her pin box in the process.

Bess grimaced at her friend and knelt to pick up all the pins from the hardwood floor with her small magnet. "He's not mean, Amber. He's actually very kind."

"To you."

Bess shrugged and placed her pin box on the side table out of Amber's range. "You just don't understand him. He's always felt guilty, is all. I try to get him to let it all go, but he blames himself for Pa and Joey's deaths."

Amber squinted and thrust her hands over her chest. "That's silly. He's not responsible for either. A person can only do their best. He ought to know that."

Bess tied off and cut the thread, weaving the excess back into the hem unseen. She sighed and frowned at her friend as she examined her stitches. "Amber, sometimes you can be needlessly cruel. He's hurting, and I understand. He's done everything he can to give me a good life." She subconsciously ran her fingers up the scars on the back of her left hand.

"Alright. I'm sorry. I don't mean to be so unfeeling." Amber shrugged. "You're right; I don't understand. Everyone has lost someone they love." The girl's lip trembled slightly, and she looked across at the photograph of her mother that hung on her wall.

Bess smiled kindly and gripped Amber's hand. "I'm sorry. I know what it's like to lose ya ma. That pain never goes away, does it?"

Amber sighed. "I wish I'd had a chance to get to know her. I was only two when she died giving birth to Coop. I only have a few vague memories of her."

Bess nodded, and her eyes flooded with tears. "I'm sorry; at least I got six years with my ma before she died."

Amber put her arm around her friend's shoulder and they lay their heads together for a time. "That's why I'm glad you're my best friend. You understand; you've lost more people than anyone."

Bess disguised her grimace, standing abruptly to hang up the complete gown. Amber's careless words often carried a sting. The pain of losing both her parents and her younger brother was still so close for Bess. She relied on God to get her through each day, but that didn't stop her from missing them. Taking a deep breath, she chose to change the subject. "Have you made a decision?"

"'Bout what?" Amber frowned, leaping up to open the wardrobe door for Bess.

"College."

Amber grimaced. "Yeah. I'm not gonna go. I'm not really interested in moving to Minneapolis. Pa has offered me a full-time job in the post office. His clerk is heading West with his brother in search of gold and fortune." She waved her arms dramatically.

Bess chuckled. "It's a good job, and it'll give you time to work out what your future holds."

The girl nodded and slumped back down. "What about you?"

"I'm going to get more work in the dress shop. I can manage half days before my hand completely packs up, then I can give some sewing or even knitting and crochet lessons to the younger girls, least the one's without ma's to teach 'em."

Amber shrugged. "It seems there are more of us than there ought to be. I don't get why God is so mean sometimes."

Bess gasped and snapped her head around. "Amber Clarke, you take that back."

Amber thrust her arms across her chest and leaned back against the wall. "No, I won't. Isn't it mean taking mas from children? You know God could'a stopped it if He wanted."

Bess frowned and tears rimmed her eyes. "God's not like that, Amber; He's not cruel and hateful. He's merciful and kind."

4

"He hasn't been kind to you. You're only sixteen, and you've been running a home since you were a girl. You're left with just a surly older brother. What kind of life have you had?"

A tear streaked down Bess's cheek. She did love Amber's forthrightness, but it really packed a punch sometimes. "Amber, I've had a wonderful life. God doesn't promise us a life free of pain or loss, but He does promise to bear it with us. I'm so grateful to him that my injury wasn't worse, and that I still have Aaron." Her lip trembled. "I have a good job at the dress shop and I have good friends." She flashed Amber a smile.

Amber chuckled. "Well yes, you ought to be grateful for me. I am the blue ribbon of friends."

Both girls laughed heartily. The post office clock chimed the hour and Bess jumped up. "Oh, I better go; I need to get supper on. I'll see you tomorrow, graduate."

Amber grinned and leaped up to hug her friend. "And you, graduate."

Bess snatched up her sewing basket and hurried down the stairs.

*   *   *   *

Aaron hurried out into the living room, in his socks, tucking his shirt into his trousers and hoisting his suspenders over his shoulders. He flicked away the wet hair plastered to his forehead and groaned as he opened the door. He flashed the young man a bemused frown. "Nate? Bess ain't here."

"I know; I just saw her go into the post office with her sewing basket." The young man gulped and looked around nervously.

"If you know she's not here, what are you doing here?"

"I ahhh.... Hmmm." The young man pursed his lips and raised his hands. "I need to talk to you for a moment. May I come in?"

Aaron shrugged and stepped aside.

Nate walked in and sat down on the couch. Aaron closed the door and took his time to walk to the armchair opposite him and sit down. He leaned back in the chair and raised his brows at Nate.

"Mr. Carter, I wanna talk to you about Bess."

Aaron frowned. "What about Bess?"

Nate took a deep breath and opted for the direct approach. He flicked his swatch of unruly brown hair back off his forehead. *I wonder if I've got time for a haircut before tomorrow.* He forced his thoughts back to the current torment. "It's probably not a shock to you that I'm rather fond of her." He couldn't help but smile.

Aaron nodded. "No, not a surprise." He knew what was coming but opted to let the boy squirm a little.

"Well, since Bess doesn't have a father, I thought... well... a man ought to do these things right, get a father's permission and all... And I figured, you're the next best thing, right?" He swallowed twice and sighed. Nate was usually very carefully spoken; he prided himself in his clever wit and his ability to communicate. But when it came to matters of the heart, it could render even the most articulate man mute.

6

"What are you saying?" Aaron played dumb and leaned forward to put his elbows on his knees.

Nate took a deep breath. "I want your permission to ask Bess to court. She's almost seventeen; she'll be done with school tomorrow."

Aaron sat back, folded his arms across his chest, and scowled. He was fine with the young man and honestly thought he'd be good for his sister, but watching Nate squirm was amusing.

He shook his head and exhaled. "She's awful young."

"I know, and it's not like I wanna marry her tomorrow; I just wanna... You know... make my intentions clear." Nate flicked his hair again.

"Which are?" Aaron pursed his lips and squinted.

Nate swallowed, exhaled loudly and grinned; a sparkle appeared in his eyes. "I love her and I plan to marry her one day, Mr. Carter."

Aaron nodded and scratched his chin, successfully keeping all emotion off his face. "I thought you were going to college in the fall?"

"I'm not sure yet. I thought I might give my pa another year or so till Micah is old enough to take on the farm chores. Give me a chance to court properly, then maybe later, when we're married, we can move to the city, and I'll go to law school like I planned. I'm not in a hurry."

Aaron nodded again. "You plan to come back here when you've graduated?"

Nate grimaced; any conversation with Aaron Carter was painful, but this one was excruciating. He sincerely hoped Aaron would put him out of his misery and give him an answer one way or another. "It would be up to Bess, but yes, I imagine so. She loves it here and so do I. I like the idea of bringing legal representation to the prairies; I think everyone deserves that right. Country folk need attorneys too."

"What makes you think you'll pass? I hear most don't." Aaron frowned at Nate. The boy was really squirming now.

"I will do everything in my power to do so, Sir. I plan to make Bess proud of me."

Aaron nodded and stared into the flames scratching his chin.

Nate raised his brows and stared at the man. He swallowed twice. The waiting was torture.

At last, Aaron turned to Nate and shrugged. "Yeah, I ain't got a problem with you asking her. It's her life."

Nate grinned; he stood up and walked to Aaron. He put his hand out. "Thank you, Sir. I promise I'll do right by her."

Aaron grimaced and stood up. He took the young man's hand and fixed his dark eyes on Nate. "You hurt her, and I'll see to it you never walk again."

Nate gulped. There was no humor in Aaron's eyes. He had absolutely no doubt that Aaron Carter would hunt him to the ends of the earth if he hurt Bess. He nodded and met Aaron's gaze. "That is the last thing I'd ever want to do. I love your sister, have since I was in the sixth grade." A wry smile crossed his face as he remembered nine-year-old Bess, a few grades below him, with rosy cheeks and long braids, skipping along the path with Amber, so carefree. He'd seen her strength through the death of her father, the fire that killed her younger brother and left her injured, and the way she'd carried on so courageously in the face of so much adversity, his love for her had grown over the years. Despite being young, he already knew she was the only woman he'd ever love for the rest of his days.

Aaron nodded. "Good."

It was a simple word, accompanied by just the slightest of smiles. From Aaron Carter, it was high praise, almost approval. Nate nodded his appreciation and strode from the house. He walked out the door, closed it behind him, and exhaled loudly. "I'm glad that's over with." He grinned and leaped off the porch, right over the stairs, climbed on his saddle horse, Mouse, and galloped away.

Two

Nate took the picnic basket from Bess and reached for the blanket, which he draped over his arm. Lifting his elbow, he grinned at her. "M'lady, will you allow me?"

Bess chuckled. "Of course, Nate."

Nate's heart flipped. Having her on his arm was thrilling. They'd been friends for a very long time, but he hoped he could change that now that she'd graduated. Nothing would please him more than to have the lovely Bess Carter on his arm for the rest of his days; well, in time, he hoped to make her Bess Sawyer.

He grinned at the thought and Bess caught it. She tilted her head to the side. "What's got you smiling like that? You're acting strange, Nate." She squinted. "I thought you said we were meeting the others."

He nodded. "We'll join the rest of your class later. I just wanted to take you on a picnic to celebrate your graduation."

"Alright." She gave him a sly grin.

They reached the common at the edge of town, where two rows of trees were planted to make an arcade. On the other side, a small arched wooden bridge crossed the lake to The Island.

The Island was a sheltered clearing amongst a group of trees. One ancient tree stood near the edge away from the others. It was a favorite spot for many in the town, and the weathered pine wore the scratched initials of many young lovers. The area was affectionately known as The Island, despite not being an actual island. It was somewhat of a peninsula that jutted out into the otherwise round lake.

The pair reached the tree and Nate laid out the blanket and gestured for Bess to sit. He placed the basket in the middle and sat down. Bess opened the basket and pulled out two tin plates and a fresh apple pie.

"That looks amazing. You're a great cook, Bess Carter."

Bess frowned. "It's a basic, everyday apple pie, Nate. I've been making them since I was small." She cut Nate a slice, and slid it onto a plate, added a spoon to the side, and passed it to him.

Nate grinned and took a bite. "It may be basic, but it's delicious. I can't even boil water; I have no idea how you manage to make flour and apples into this masterpiece."

Bess shook her head. "Men! You really do get worked up over pie. My brother is the same. All I have to do to placate him is whip out a pie, and I could persuade him to do almost anything."

Nate scowled. "Wish I'd known that yesterday," he mumbled.

"Yesterday? What do you mean?"

"Oh, nothing, just talking to myself." He took another large bite, winked at her, and swallowed it.

Bess took a much smaller bite and then laid her plate down. She looked around at the scene. It was a bright June day; happy birds twittered around, wildflowers grew in abundance and the world seemed to smile on them. "This is such a beautiful place. I'm not surprised so many weddings happen out here." She sounded almost wistful.

Nate nodded and stored that information away in his memory. He'd be just fine with marrying Bess out here under the pine. He'd marry her in the kitchen if she wanted. He took another bite and tried to keep the blush from his cheeks. "Yes." He swallowed his too large mouthful and coughed. "It is beautiful, here." He grew bold then and looked up at her. "Not as beautiful as you in that gown." He looked her up and down. The blush pink dress complemented her rosy cheeks and full lips. Her dark hair shone in the sunlight, and he couldn't help but admire the ivory of her skin.

Bess blushed and bit her lips together. "Nate."

Nate put down his plate and reached for one gloved hand. "I mean it, Bess, you're a beautiful girl... uh... woman."

Bess's cheeks colored deeply. "Thank you." She gulped, feeling her heart rate increase. She looked up at him shyly.

"When I saw you on that stage this morning, collecting your diploma, I just about fainted. I was glad I was sitting down."

"Oh, Nate, don't be silly. I'm just the same old Bess you've been at school with since I was in the fourth grade."

"Nope, not true, that was a pretty little girl. You're a beautiful woman now."

She sighed and hung her head. "Nate, I'm damaged."

Nate reached over and lifted her chin. He furrowed his brow and searched her face. "What? Why would you say that?"

She lifted her injured hand, hidden by the long white glove, and sighed.

Nate reached for the hand and, tugging at the fingers of the glove, he slipped it off. He held the injured hand in his large ones. "Bess, you're not damaged." He traced the scar that ran over her hand and partway up her forearm. "There is beauty in these scars."

Bess sighed. "Beauty? Look, they're purple and uneven. My hand gets stiff and my fingers sore. It's never been the same since the fire."

Nate dared to reach up and tuck a strand of hair behind her ear. It made her gasp. His touch was so soft. Her heart rate increased a little more and her cheeks warmed. Nate looked into her clear blue eyes and lifted the hand to his lips. He kept holding it as he lowered it and turned it over in his hand again. "This hand is beautiful to me. It reminds me of all you've faced and borne up under and how strong and lovely you are. You have not an ounce of bitterness or hate over any of it. Which is more than I can say for your brother."

Bess pulled her hand away and sighed. "Don't say that. Aaron has a lot on his shoulders."

"I know, but so do you. I'm proud of you, Bess, from the young girl who came to town not long after losing your mother, to watching you go through the loss of your father. I know you took care of your brothers and kept the house even at that age. Then when the fire happened, I thought you'd never return to school. I

13

remember it clearly. I was fourteen and I heard that you were in the hospital in Minneapolis. I missed your smile, and your beautiful eyes. I'd never thought that about a girl before. That was four years ago, and I've watched you persevere and grow into this beautiful young woman."

"Nate." Bess's lips trembled. "You've always had a way with words."

"They aren't just words, Bess...."

She raised her brows.

He swallowed, reached for the hand again, and gave her a kind smile. "It's love."

Bess sucked in a breath. "What are you saying?"

"I'm saying, I want you to be my girl. I wanna call on you."

Bess's eyes flooded with tears. "Oh, Nate, please don't ask me."

He frowned. "Bess, I love you. I have since the sixth grade, as much as a boy can when he's eleven. That love has grown all these years. And now that you've graduated and you're a woman, free to make your way in the world. I..." He shrugged and raised a hand to her cheek. He smiled at her with his whole face. "I want us to court. I plan to marry you someday, Bess Carter."

Bess closed her eyes and tears streamed down her cheeks. "Nate..." she opened them again and they pleaded with him to stop. "I... don't know what to say."

He leaned in and kissed her cheek, brushing the other with his knuckles. "Say yes. It's okay if you don't love me yet; I know you will in time. We can have a wonderful life. I wanna go to law school in a few years time, after we're married, and we can have a practice in the city, or here or wherever you want to go."

Bess creased her brows. "Nate, I care for you so. You are a dear, dear man and a friend I treasure so...."

He nodded and frowned. "But just a friend?"

"Oh, Nate, I want to say yes to you. You have no idea how much I want to say yes to you...." Tears rolled down her cheeks.

"Then say yes...."

Her tears increased. She stood and walked to the large pine and leaned back against it. "I can't."

Nate leaped up to follow her, the discarded pie long forgotten. "Why?"

"Nate, you should go to college, get your law degree, make something of yourself and forget about me."

"Bess Carter, I will never forget about you. One doesn't extinguish love like it's a lantern."

"I can't do this right now, Nate." Her lips trembled. "Please know I care for you, very much."

Nate's face curled up and he fought desperately to stop his broken heart from escaping his eyes as tears. "What's this all about? You say you want to say yes. What's stopping you?"

"I'm just not ready, Nate. We are so young, and I don't know what God has planned for me. I only just finished school, and, ohhhh...." She couldn't keep the tremble from her lips.

Nate walked away two paces and turned his back on her. He took a deep breath and nodded. Turning back, he gripped her hand again. "Okay. I'll wait, just as long as it takes. I'll go to college. I'll get my law degree, and

I'll make you proud of me, and then when I ask you again, I hope you'll say yes to me."

Bess bit her lips again and gave him a single nod.

"That's hope at least." He smiled. "Will you at least write to me? I want to get to know you even more; every last morsel of information will be music to my heart."

"Oh, Nate, your words are so eloquent. I don't know how to speak or write like you. I can't imagine why you're even interested in me." She grimaced and hung her head.

He lifted her chin and nodded. "I'm a great deal more than interested. I'm enamored, intrigued, and head over heels in love with you, Bess. But I'll wait. I'll wait as long as you want me to, as long as there is hope."

She gave him another nod and a sad smile.

He raised his brows. "Promise you'll write?"

"Of course, we're friends, aren't we?"

"If that's all I can have for now, then friends it is. Good, close, dear friends."

"I'd like that." She smiled.

Nate could see the tremble to her lips, and it looked like she was going to cry again. He reached for her and wrapped her in a warm embrace. "It's okay. Bess, my heart is yours alone, and when you're ready to give me yours, I'll be waiting. And I can promise you it'll always be safe with me." He took a deep breath and laid his cheek against her hair. Her scent was tantalizing. He couldn't place the fragrance, but he etched it in his memory.

She stepped back from him and gave him a shy smile.

Nate took her hand and led her back to the picnic spot. They gathered their things. "M'lady." He put his arm out to her again. She hesitated. "Friends can link arms, Bess."

She smiled. "Okay."

Nate led her back toward town to meet her classmates. On the outside, he was calm and accepting, but inside, his heart was doing its utmost not to shatter. Still, she hadn't said an outright no, not ever, just that she wanted to wait. He could respect that. She was very young. *I mean what I said. I'll wait, Bess; one day, I'll make you my wife, but I'll wait, just as long as you need me to.*

Three

Bess swiped a tear off her cheek as she leaned back against the rough leather seat and dropped Nate's latest missive on the floor of the slow-moving train. It'd been five months since that day, on The Island when she'd refused him, and as the train inched towards Chicago, she trembled.

So much had happened since Nate left for the University of Illinois, three months prior. They'd been corresponding since and he'd written faithfully almost every week.

In his last letter, he'd told her about the cotillions he'd attended. It seemed he'd got in with a wealthy lot in Chicago and had been invited to dances and plays and all sorts of events that were part of the lifestyle of the wealthy. His life sounded so interesting, yet so peculiar at the same time.

She wasn't going to Chicago to see Nate, if she had it her way, she'd never step a toe out of Minnesota, but her sick aunt had asked her to come so she might get to know her before she passed.

The thought of being in the same city as Nate was both exhilarating and terrifying. His letter said next time he saw her, he'd ask her again. She sighed. "Lord, help me to keep my wits about me; he's so wonderful, so handsome, so charming and...." She exhaled loudly and closed her eyes. "And so not a Christian." She sighed again. "Help me when I see him to keep my nerve. I know it isn't right to be yoked together with an

18

unbeliever." Despite her resolve, the deep longing in her heart had never gone away.

She was in love with Nate, she'd known that for a long time, even when she was a girl. But her faith was everything to her, and serving the Lord was her utmost priority. Tears streaked down her cheeks, and she raised her handkerchief to her eyes. "Oh, Lord, help me with my feelings, or better still, bring Nate to salvation. I love him so." Her trembling lips dared speak the words aloud. She was grateful Cousin Frederick had given her a private cabin on the train; this was hardly dignified behavior for a lady in public. She wiped her tears and quoted. "Be ye not unequally yoked together with unbelievers: for what fellowship hath righteousness with unrighteousness? And what communion hath light with darkness?"

"Lord, I know what is right, and I know You call us to lay aside our worldly desires to seek after You. Help me to lay aside Nate, no matter how much I love him. Help me to give him up, to not dream of what a future with him might look like, to not plead with You to make it happen when I know that it is wrong.

"I trust that You have planned my future and You hold me in Your hands." She took a deep breath and smiled, despite her tears. "Yes, I'm prepared to lay aside my feelings for Nate. I'll live the life of a spinster if You ask it of me. But I sure am gonna need Your help, Lord."

A knock on her door cut her prayer short. "Coming." She brushed at her eyes, picked up the letter, and forced her emotions deep inside. Standing carefully on the lurching train, she opened the cabin door.

"Just thought you might like some breakfast, Ma'am. It's complimentary to all our first-class passengers." The young boy walked in at her bidding and laid the tray on her table.

"Thank you, that's most kind. Do you know if we are on schedule? I have someone waiting for me in Chicago."

"Yes, Ma'am, due to arrive at ten a.m. as specified. You want coffee with that?"

"Yes, thank you." Bess smiled at the boy; he couldn't have been much more than twelve.

He hurried out to the cart in the corridor, poured her a cup, and walked back in, clearly used to balancing in the jostling train. "Enjoy your breakfast, Ma'am."

"Thank you...?" She raised her brows.

"Joey, Ma'am, the name's Joey."

Bess blinked back a tear. "That was my younger brother's name, he's passed now, but you remind me of him."

"I'm sorry, Ma'am."

"Thank you, Joey, and thank you for breakfast."

With a nod, the boy was gone, pushing his cart to the next cabin.

Bess closed the door and chuckled. "Ma'am? I'm only seventeen." She sat down before the tray and picked up a fork. Saying a quick prayer of gratitude for the food, she ate heartily, only now realizing just how hungry she was.

* * * *

Nate drummed his fingers on the table and sighed loudly. Henry Martin looked up at him and scowled. "Quit the drumming, Sawyer. This is a library."

Nate grimaced at him and picked up his pen. He sighed again, put the pen back down, laid his elbow on the table, and rested his head on his hand.

Tim Daniels dropped his pen and raised his brows from across the table. "We got an exam tomorrow, Sawyer. You better get studying."

"It's no good; I can't concentrate."

Henry grinned. "What's on your mind?"

"As if you don't know." Tim rolled his eyes and grinned.

"Besssss," Henry teased and made kissing noises.

Nate furrowed his brows but couldn't keep the blush from his cheeks. He ran his fingers through his unruly hair. Finally he grinned. "She's always on my mind."

A stern librarian walked past and scowled at them, peering over her spectacles at them, and putting a finger to her lips.

The three gentlemen frowned at each other, shook their heads, and turned back to their books.

Nate turned a page and picked up his pen to take notes. He read the same paragraph three times and sighed. Thrusting the book closed louder than he meant to, he caught the librarian's eye and cringed. "It's no good, chaps. I can't concentrate. I need to get out of here."

His two friends looked up, nodded, and joined him, slipping their books into their satchels and hurrying out the door. At last, they stepped out into the cool October air. Henry shivered. "Where do you wanna go?"

"Thought I might head for the park and take a walk."

Both Nate's friends rolled their eyes.

"What is it with you and walking in the wilderness?" Henry scoffed.

"He's a country boy, you know that. Comes from the prairies." Tim laughed aloud.

Nate brushed off their mocking. "Can't deny it. I love the open spaces, can't quite get used to the noises of the city."

"I was born and raised here. There's no place in the world like Chicago." Tim fell into step with his two friends.

"Me too. Helps that we come from the finest families in town. I'll never tire of being rich." Henry grinned.

Nate shrugged his shoulders. "Wouldn't know. I'm the son of a farmer."

Tim tipped his head to the side and scratched his chin. "How'd you afford to come here anyway?"

Nate grimaced. "Scholarship. Our pastor endorsed me. The college took pity on me, I guess."

"Well, I wish you'd come and live with me at my estate. We have twelve bedrooms, only five of them are used. We have space, Nate."

Nate nodded. "It's a generous offer, I couldn't accept."

"Why not?" Tim frowned. "You can't get a nicer home than the Martin Estate, 'sides it's only just round the corner. Gotta be better than that dingy old boarding house."

22

Nate shrugged. "I'm fine where I am. I like living there, the lady that runs it is nice, and I get my meals prepared for me. In truth, she reminds me of my ma."

"Ma. It's so quaint how you country folk talk." Henry slapped him on the back. "I will admit you're well-spoken for a country boy, but sometimes I can hear the farmer in you."

"Thanks, I think." Nate frowned.

"Well, give it some thought. Father told me to ask you. He likes you."

Nate tilted his head at Henry and flicked his hair back off his face. "He's only met me twice."

"Yeah, but he's a good judge of character. I think he likes you because you're honest. In his line of work, he deals with a lot of corrupt men, out to swindle people and do whatever they can to make a dollar. He can see right through them."

"I promised I'll think about it. Now if you don't mind, I think I'll go back to my room and write a letter." Nate's eyes glistened, and he bit his lip to keep his grin at bay.

"To Besssssss," the two gentlemen said in unison.

Nate was not one to be easily bated. "Least I got someone to write to. Don't see any young ladies hovering around you two eligible bachelors."

Tim frowned and scratched his chin. "Yeah, but she turned you down. Why are you still bothering with her? There are a lot of elegant specimens in this town." He winked to a group of young ladies who walked past. They gave him a glare and hurried away.

"Because I love her. I can't just turn that off. She wasn't ready, and I understand, but I'll be ready and waiting whenever she is." Nate sighed. "I miss her. She's the loveliest girl I know."

Henry stroked his chin and shook his head. He furrowed his brows at Nate. "Quaint! All this falling in love."

"You don't believe in falling in love?" Nate rubbed his chin and squinted at Henry.

Tim shrugged one shoulder and answered on Henry's behalf. "It's not how we do it in our set. Usually, our match is arranged for us. Doesn't matter if you love them or not; a good match between prestigious families is more important. Guarantees a stable life."

Nate frowned. "But what if you don't even like them?"

Henry shrugged. "Doesn't matter. My folks never liked each other much. They sleep in separate rooms these days, but they make it work."

"How is that making it work? I can't imagine ever courting a woman I didn't love. I'd rather live in a cave to have Bess's love than marry for riches with a woman I didn't like."

Tim nodded. "Quaint." He lifted his eyes to Henry, but he thought about Nate's words. "I like how you think, though. I guess when you don't have money it's not everything to you. You have different priorities."

"Yeah, my parents do okay as far as farmers go. Just had Micah and me, and we worked hard our whole lives, but it's a good life, and one day I plan to go back to

Robertson Township, marry Bess and live happily ever after."

Henry shook his head. "You are a country boy."

"That's why you like me though, right?"

"Something like that, Sawyer. See, this is why you ought to come and live with me; we'll knock some of the country boy out of you and teach you how to live like a gentleman." Henry patted his back.

"I said I'll think about it." Nate stopped walking outside a green door. "Well, I'll see you chaps tomorrow. Let's hope we pass the test."

"I will." Tim grinned. "I don't have a lady on my mind."

Henry scowled. "You always have ladies on your mind."

"Yeah, all the ladies, not just one."

Nate and Henry shook their heads. Nate waved as he turned to walk through the heavy door.

Four

"Knowles will be here at three to take you to town, Miss."

"Thank you, Crews, that's most kind." Bess smiled at the butler.

Crews nodded and left the room.

"Aunt Mere, do you want to come with me today?"

"Oh, I don't think so, Bess, Dear. I'm feeling a bit weak today."

"Aunt Mere, you are stronger than you think."

The older woman nodded and reached a gnarled hand across to touch Bess's arm. "I feel stronger with you here. I'm so glad you came. You've adjusted very well in two weeks."

"Thank you. When I first stepped through the door, I couldn't believe how vast and elegant this place was. It's like a palace."

Meredith laughed. "Hardly, but I thank you, Dear."

Bess smiled and sipped at her tea.

"You really look the part; you could be a debutante. We can have a coming out for you next season; you're so lovely, you'd make a wonderful match."

"Oh, Aunt Mere. I'm not a city debutante; I'm just a farm girl, in city clothing." Bess shrugged.

"Not anymore, Bess. You're an heiress, remember."

Bess blushed deeply. "Aunty, I can't accept your offer; it's much too generous. We've just got to know one another, and you don't owe me any...."

Meredith raised her hand and pursed her lips, stopping Bess abruptly. "No, Bess, you deserve it. It's only what was rightfully your mother's inheritance. Thirty percent of the current worth of the estate, cash and landholdings, and the cottage on the other side of town, that used to be my grandparent's home. It includes twenty-two acres of land and forest. It's yours and your brother's to do with as you please."

Bess's lips trembled and she looked up at her aunt with tears in her eyes. "It's most generous of you. I feel so bad about accepting it when I've done nothing at all to earn it."

"That's not true, Bess. Just having you here with me is a blessing. You're helping me go through my affairs and your mother's things, all that belonged to Mother and Father. I couldn't be more grateful. Frederick has no desire to do any of that." The older woman shrugged. "Besides, he's too busy with his father's business."

Bess smiled and squeezed her aunt's arm. "I'm glad to be here. It's very overwhelming for me, but I am so enjoying getting to know Ma more through you."

Meredith sighed. "Never a day goes by when I don't think about my sister. Luella was always an independent spirit. She turned her nose up at tradition. Didn't have a coming out, refused to be betrothed to the man Father wanted her to marry, fell in love with the help." She shook her head and chuckled. "And you are just like her. I nearly fainted when I laid eyes on you. You are certainly your mother's daughter. And a lot like my mother." Mere lifted her eyebrows, gesturing to a portrait on the wall.

Bess smiled. "My pa told me that once, that I was like Ma and her ma."

"Well, it's true, Dear. You keep saying you want to get to know your mother. Start by looking in the mirror and inside yourself; you'll find a lot of her there."

Both women turned their heads when Frederick entered the room.

"Afternoon, Ladies." He bent down to kiss his mother on the cheek and nodded to Bess. He slumped into the armchair next to her.

"You're home early today, Son."

"Yeah, I've just come to offer Bess an invitation."

Bess looked up incredulously. "Me?"

"Yes, you."

"Invitation to what?"

"A cotillion, this evening."

Bess's eyes flew up. "Oh, I... I don't know what to say. I don't have anything to wear to a cotillion."

"Oh, don't worry about that, we'll have Sophie arrange for Mrs. Sullivan to send a selection of gowns this evening, and you can pick out what you want."

"Aunt Mere, I can't let you do that for me."

Mere raised her brows. "You are an heiress of this estate, Bess, and you must dress and behave accordingly. Besides, you can afford it and so can I. You don't have to feel bad about spending money. We have plenty."

Bess gave her a wry smile. The older woman didn't mean to sound snobbish, it was just the lifestyle she was accustomed to. *I must really be my mother's daughter, I see why she left. All this decadence makes me feel uneasy. What the people back home would think of me.* She blushed. *I could buy all of Robertson Township five times over with what this place is worth.*

"Very well, I should very much enjoy attending a cotillion. Am I to have an escort?" Bess grinned at her aunt.

Meredith smiled and nodded, glad to see Bess was coming around to the customs of the station. It had been hard enough to insist she get a whole new wardrobe and to even get her out of the house. "I'm glad to hear you speaking like that. You sound like an heiress already."

"Oh, Aunty. I won't even inherit until you pass, and that is some time away yet."

"No, my dear, I signed the paperwork yesterday when my lawyer was here. It's already all yours. And yes, I feel good at the moment; my doctor is optimistic that I might have more time than he thought. But even if I live twenty more years, I still want you to have what should rightfully have belonged to Luella. Father wanted it that way. Had he a son, everything would have gone to him, but with two daughters, he insisted my husband and I have two-thirds share, and Arthur took over the business, and Lu as the younger was to have a third."

Bess could do little more than nod. "How do you feel about the arrangement, Fred?"

The young man smiled at her. "It's not up to me, and it's right. I want you to have it. And to answer your question. I will be your escort. It would be my pleasure."

"I'd like that, thank you. But don't you have a young lady you want to take?"

Aunt Mere let out a guttural groan. "If only. I've been trying to encourage Frederick to find a wife; the manor will need a new Mrs. Bennett in time. He's already nearly twenty-five and it's high time he settled down. But he doesn't seem interested in any of the young ladies that hang around."

Fred closed his eyes and sighed. He opened them and fixed his eyes on his mother. "I won't marry someone who only wants my money."

"We could find you a lovely girl if you want to. You know Mr. Calvin Watson is looking at you for his daughter. She's a sweet girl."

Fred exhaled loudly. "Caroline Watson is awfully mean. Besides, she's barely sixteen. I'm twenty-four. That would be obscene."

"Why does that matter? Marriage isn't about age or love; it's about station and prestige."

"I'm well aware of the expectations, Mother," Frederick said through gritted teeth. "I'll marry when I'm good and ready. In the meantime..." He turned to smile at his cousin. "It would be my pleasure to take you to a cotillion. It will be a nice change to not have someone fawning over me just for my money."

"Well, I certainly won't do that, Cousin Fred."

"I must get back to work. Be ready at eight o'clock and I'll have Knowles come for you. I'll meet you at the hall. Sorry I can't accompany you there. I have back-to-back meetings with my executives, but I'll be outside waiting for you at precisely eight-thirty."

"That's very good." Bess gasped. "Oh, I must go see to my errand. I'll be back around five, Aunty. Are you sure there isn't anything you need?"

"No, Dear, but I'll have the dresses ready for you to select from when you get back."

Bess gripped her aunt's shoulder as she hurried to meet the carriage out front.

* * * *

"You dress up okay for a country boy," Henry teased.

Nate turned to glance at himself in the mirror. "Thank you. I feel a little out of place in this expensive suit." He gestured to the jacket and top hat waiting on the bed for him.

"You look the part." Henry's sister Annabelle wandered in. "No one would ever guess you're from the prairies." She touched his arm flirtatiously.

Nate flinched and stepped away from her. "It's most kind of you all to lend me these clothes." He changed the subject.

Henry turned from adjusting his cravat in the mirror. "Lend? They're yours, Chap. You're gonna need fine clothing if you're going to make it as a city attorney."

"I don't plan to be a city attorney. I told you. I plan to go home...."

"I know and marry Bess. But Miss Bess isn't here and Annabelle is, and so are many other charming young ladies, and, at least, while you are here, we deserve the chance to try to change your mind."

31

Nate shook his head at them. He didn't mind escorting Annabelle to Cotillions, but he longed for Bess. *What I wouldn't give to take Bess to a cotillion, see her dressed up and waltzing in the low lamplight.* "Well, I appreciate you including a poor country boy in your life. You've all been most kind to me."

"We like you, Nate. You're an honest and good chap." Henry slapped his back.

"Thank you."

Five

Fred opened the carriage door and grinned. He put his hand out to help Bess down. She lifted her skirts and took his outstretched hand, trying desperately not to fall down the stairs in the new shoes. The heels were much higher than she was used to. Once she was on solid ground, she dropped her dress and brushed the pale green silk back into place, cringing at the wrinkles in the hem.

"You look lovely, Bess."

"Thank you, Cousin. I feel so hopelessly out of place. This dress is just about worth more than our entire farm back home. It really is a frivolous expense, and I feel more than a little silly." She grimaced and glanced down at the elegant pale green gown, with thousands of shimmering beads. She pulled her thin shawl around her shoulders. The capped sleeves were elegant, but she was chilly and glad she'd opted for long gloves. They'd serve two purposes, hiding the scars and keeping her warm.

"You aren't silly, Bess."

"No, and I haven't forgotten who I am. This is not me; it's just a role I'm playing. I'm just Bess Carter from Robertson Township, Minnesota. I'm not a city deb." She closed her eyes. "Oh, this is all wrong. I shouldn't be here pretending to be someone I'm not."

"Why not, Bess? Why can't you be at a cotillion in a nice dress and still be Bess Carter of Robertson

Township, Minnesota? It doesn't change who you are on the inside. Only you can do that."

"Thank you. You're right, Cousin. I am still just Bess, and I haven't forgotten who I am. But God has blessed me so abundantly in this season of my life. And I will be gracious and accept His blessing, but I'll be sure to use it to bless others."

Fred grinned. "I find you rather inspirational. You have your head screwed on right. I'm glad you're here. I feel I could learn a lot from you."

Bess raised her brows. "From me? What could you possibly learn from me?"

"More than you'd know, Bess. You're a smart, and lovely girl. Not unlike your mother, from what I hear."

"That's what they tell me." Bess shivered.

"Come on, let's go in before you catch your death of cold. It's much easier for us chaps; we get to wear suit jackets. I feel for ladies with thin fabrics and exposed skin." He gestured to the low neckline.

Bess nodded and took his arm.

"Wow," she couldn't help but exclaim as they walked in. The room was a whirl with color and decorations, food, and music. She thought about the dances back home and chuckled. This was a far cry from a church social.

Fred stopped at the door and Bess gave him a quizzical look.

Fred leaned his head in and whispered, "We need to be presented." He passed the doorman a card. The stiff-backed man looked at it briefly and announced, "Mr. Frederick Bennet and Miss Elizabeth Carter." He nodded to them and they entered the room as the man greeted the next couple.

*   *   *   *

Nate escorted Annabelle over to the beverage stand. "May I get you a drink, Miss Martin?"

"No, you know how it is. You're only my excuse to get here. Father won't let me come without an escort. Now, you make yourself scarce and don't come near me until the carriage returns." She grinned at Nate, she liked him well enough, but this was the only way she could be with her true love, Ross Neil. He wasn't of their family's class and her father disapproved of him, so they met at cotillions whenever they could.

Nate nodded and wandered over to Henry and Tim, talking to a group of young men. A waitress brought them each a glass of wine and they nodded their thank you and fell into conversation.

"So, any young ladies caught your eye?" Henry nudged his friend.

Tim looked around. Noticing the beautiful woman who stepped in on Frederick Bennet's arm, he grinned. "I like the look of her."

"Mr. Frederick Bennet and Miss Elizabeth Carter." The voice echoed through the room.

Nate's head flicked up and his eyes grew wide. He pivoted on his heels and looked towards the door. Henry and Tim raised eyebrows at each other as Nate's face lit up. His eyes misted over. "Bess," he whispered, unable to drag his eyes off her.

"Bess?" The two other men looked at each other. "She's here?" Henry's mouth dropped open.

Tim's eyes grew wide. "That's Bess?"

Nate grinned. "Yes."

"I can see why you like her. What are you gonna do about Bennett?" Tim grimaced.

Nate grinned. "I'm not worried about, Bennett; he's her cousin." He put his glass down and raised his brows. His heart was doing somersaults and his face warmed up. "I can't believe she's here. I'm dreaming, aren't I, chaps? I'm going to wake up any moment."

* * * *

Bess froze. She felt eyes on her and flicked her head up. "Nate?" She lifted one gloved hand to her mouth and gasped. Her heart began to speed up and her cheeks grew hot. "Oh, Nate." Tears flooded her eyes. *What is he doing here? I wasn't quite ready to see him yet, Lord.* The tumultuous feelings she thought she had under control flooded back to her. She blushed as he approached, almost in slow motion.

He reached her and they looked at each other for a time, oblivious to all those dancing around them. Neither spoke. Bess lowered her eyes. "Hello."

He reached a hand out to lift her chin. He grinned, his eyes exploring her face. "Bess. What are you doing here?"

She smiled. "My cousin brought me." She shrugged and gestured to Fred, who'd stepped back from her.

"No, I mean, what are you doing in Chicago?"

Bess could hear very little over her pounding heart. The way he looked at her almost made her knees crumble. "I came to stay with my aunt." Her lips trembled.

Nate reached for her hand, lifted it to his lips and kissed it, despite the glove. "Well, I sure am glad you're here." He took her other hand and looked her in the eye. "I can't believe it. I thought I was dreaming."

"Nate." Tears sprung to the corners of her eyes.

"What is it?" He frowned; they were in a noisy, crowded room. "Come on, let's go outside." He gripped her hand and led her through the crowd. Bess numbly allowed herself to be led.

He took her through the French doors and onto a wide covered balcony. She walked over and peered over the railing at the lights of the city. Her lips trembled and her eyes glistened with tears.

"Bess?" Nate touched her arm and she turned to look at him. "What is it?

"I wasn't expecting to see you here; it just caught me off guard."

"But what's with the tears?" He gently brushed an escapee off her cheek. "Aren't you pleased to see me?" He frowned.

"Of course. I was going to come and find you next week, before your birthday."

Nate flashed her his wide, slow smile. It made her heart flutter. She fought with all her might to not throw herself in his arms and cry that she loved him.

"I'm beyond glad you're here. How long will you be in the city for?" It wasn't the question he wanted to ask, but he'd get to it.

She shrugged. "I don't really know. My aunt is dying; she has cancer."

"Ohhh." Nate was genuinely touched. He squeezed her arm compassionately.

"She asked me to come to get to know her. She is my mother's older sister, and she wanted to spend time with me, with us really, but Aaron didn't want to come."

"I'm not surprised; your brother is hardly a ray of sunshine."

"Nate." She sighed.

"I'm sorry, so you'll be here 'til...."

"At least until she passes. I don't know how long that will be, but I've given her my word I'll stay and help my cousin settle the estate. She's left me... well, some things that belonged to my mother." She didn't want him knowing about the inheritance yet; her resolve was crumbling as it was.

Nate grinned again. "I'm over the moon. Now that I know you're in town, I'm not going to be able to focus on anything."

"Nate."

"You are so beautiful; you quite literally stopped me in my tracks in there." He winked and lifted her hand.

"Oh, Nate. You're too kind."

Leaning in, he brushed her cheek, then whispered in her ear, "It's true; you're the most beautiful woman I know, with or without the fancy dress."

She bit her lip and gave him a sad smile.

"Come on, dance with me. I must dance with the prettiest girl in the room. The chaps are gonna be awful jealous of their prairie friend now."

"I'd like to. But I don't know all the steps to the dances." Bess furrowed her brow.

Nate craned his neck to listen. "Well, this one's just a waltz. You know that one."

"Alright." She smiled and allowed herself to be led to the dance floor. They picked up the rhythm quickly. "You've got good at this." She beamed as he nimbly led her around the floor.

"Only because I'm with you."

"Nate." She blushed and lowered her eyes. He explored her face while they danced, quite unable to believe she was really there.

Henry nudged Tim and nodded towards Nate. "Look how he looks at her. He really is in love with her."

Tim looked up at the pair and chuckled. "Can't keep his eyes off her. Yep, she'll be his before you can blink."

"She's a beautiful woman. I can see why he likes her."

Tim nodded. "Prettiest girl in here and least amount of make-up and foibles."

"And far too good for a country boy like him." Henry shook his head, and Tim roared with laughter.

A slow song began, and Nate pulled Bess closer. They danced in silence for several songs, and then Nate could stand it no more.

"Bess?"

"Mmhhmm." She looked up at him. The love in his eyes made her gasp. Her resolve was becoming dangerously thin, and dancing in his arms made it worse.

"Are you really pleased to see me?"

"Of course, Nate." She smiled.

He raised his brows. "Pleased enough to take me up on my offer?"

"What offer?"

He leaned in and whispered in her ear. "To court."

Bess gasped and closed her eyes. She dropped his hands and ran from the dance floor back out to the balcony.

Not your finest moment, Nathaniel! So much for broaching the subject gently.

Nate walked out after her. Bess was standing overlooking the city again. One gloved hand at her neck. She gulped in breaths and fought the tears with all her might.

"Bess, is everything okay?" He put his hand out to her shoulder. She sighed loudly. "Bess?" His voice was tender and caring. "Look at me."

She obliged, and in the low lantern light, he noticed the tears in her eyes and the tremble of her lips.

He fixed his eyes on her. "You didn't answer my question."

"What question?" The heat rose in her cheeks, and her heart raced.

He stroked her cheek. "I love you. Will you be my girl? I told you in my letter I'd ask you again."

"Please don't ask me. I might lose my resolve and give in." She bit her lips and closed her eyes, dropping her chin to her chest. Her heart pounded loudly in her ears. She wanted nothing more than to give her heart to Nate. But ohhh, Scripture made it very clear – *Be ye not unequally yoked together with unbelievers; for what fellowship hath righteousness with unrighteousness? And what communion hath light with darkness?* The verse rang in her ears. She sighed deeply, and her lips trembled.

Nate took a deep breath and sucked back his emotions. "I won't ask, for now. But may I know why?"

She raised tear-filled eyes to meet his. Heat filled her cheeks. She swallowed and her lips trembled. "I've told you why, in my letters, every time you asked."

He raised his brows. "The unequally yoked thing?"

Bess nodded, the tears threatening again at any moment. She hung her head, unable to look in his eyes. The hurt and longing she saw there was unbearable.

Nate furrowed his brows and put a hand out to gently lift her chin. Her blue eyes met his gaze, and tears pooled in the corners. He could feel her face trembling in his hands.

He sighed. "You know I love you, right?"

Bess bit her lip and nodded twice. A tear escaped. She swallowed.

"And you love me, don't you?"

She closed her eyes. The pleading in his eyes was too much to bear. *Be ye not unequally yoked together with unbelievers.* Bess closed her eyes as the tears overflowed.

Nate cupped her cheek tenderly in his large hand. "Bess?"

She opened her eyes to him. "Please don't make me say it."

Nate nodded, swallowed, and dropped his hand. He sighed loudly and took a few steps away from her. He just needed a moment. *Why does that matter so much to her? So, I'm not religious like she is, but I'd never stop her from going to church. I like that about her, that she has faith in something so much bigger than herself.*

Bess was openly weeping now. Nate walked to her and dared to take her into his arms while she cried. He lay his head on hers and drank deeply of her scent. *Wild Jasmine.*

At last, she stopped crying and stepped back from him. She lifted her handkerchief to her eyes.

"So, if I was a Christian, you'd let me come courting?"

"Yes, of course."

Nate tilted his head and scratched at his chin. He closed his eyes and sighed. "I want to believe, Bess."

"What's stopping you?"

He shrugged one shoulder. "God hasn't done anything for me. I've had to work hard to get where I am." He eyed Bess and picked up her weak hand. He pulled the top of her glove down to reveal some of the scars. "I'm not sure I could follow a God that would let so much suffering happen to such a lovely girl."

Bess's brows creased; she dared to reach up and put her hand on his chest. "God allows bad things to happen to even the best of people. I can't change that. But He also walks beside me every day and helps me to bear it all. He helps me to love and to worship Him."

Nate sighed and turned his back on her. "I don't think I can believe like you do."

"I'll pray for you."

He turned to look at her, his eyes pleading. "I'd never stop you from going to church. I love that you have a strong faith in God. I admire it and envy it. I wish I could trust in something so completely like you do. I just don't understand it." He raised his hand to her cheek again. "We could still court; I'm honorable, you know that."

Nate paused and looked her in the eye. He leaned in a little and she didn't back away, so he lowered his head and brought his lips to hers in a gentle, soft kiss. *What did you do that for? Now she'll never trust you!* He looked down at her raised face, eyes tightly closed and a charming blush to her cheeks. She opened her mouth slightly and exhaled, opening her eyes to look at him. She trembled.

"I'm sorry, Bess."

She smiled shyly at him. "Don't be." Her voice was soft and dreamy. "That was very nice."

He smiled and brushed her cheek. "I'm in love with you, Bess Carter. Won't you let me call on you? Please? I know you love me too. You were as implicit in that kiss as I was." He raised his brows at her.

"I can't, Nate. I want to. Can't you see?" Her face curled up in agony. "I want nothing more than to give you my heart..." She sucked in a breath. "But, I can't. It's not right." Her tears came again.

Nate sucked in a breath and folded his arms across his chest. He wouldn't say he was angry, but hurt and confused. "So basically, you are saying you love God more than you love the idea of courting me?"

Bess smiled through her tears and raised a hand to his cheek. "Nate, God is the most important person in my life. He always will be. He means everything to me, is involved in every decision I make, and I live to do my utmost to honor Him. That hasn't changed, even here in the city." She paused. "I could never marry a man who didn't share the most important part of my life." She grimaced and dropped her hand. "And I could never court a man I couldn't marry."

Nate paused for a time, closed his eyes, and took a deep breath. "But if I was to become a Christian, you'd agree to court?"

"If you became a Christian for the right reasons."

He frowned. "What do you mean?"

"God knows the heart, Nate. He'd know if you only pretended to believe in Him just so we could court. This is never going to change for me. God will always be my foremost love. I need you to understand that and share it with me." She shrugged. "Or I could never court...." She hung her head again and whispered, "No matter how much I love you."

He took a deep breath, and Bess could see the hurt in his eyes. He nodded twice and swallowed back the tears that threatened. "Then, I'll be going." He turned to walk back into the dance. "Goodnight."

"Nate, please don't leave like this." Her tears overflowed again. "I don't mean to hurt you."

He spun on his heels and flashed sad eyes at her. "Don't you?"

She closed her eyes and a sob escaped her lips. "I have to be true to my God, Nate."

"I understand." His hurting eyes searched hers. "But I won't stand around and wait for you to come to your senses." He was uncharacteristically harsh – it was the hurt talking. "You can't come crawling back when you change your mind." He sucked in two breaths. His words had hurt her, and he could see the tremble in her lips. He knew she was trying to keep her cool.

"Do you have to go? I hoped we could spend more time together?"

He shrugged. "Why?"

She screwed up her face. "Nate, we are friends, aren't we?"

He shook his head, and a tear ran down his cheek, despite his best efforts. He swiped at it with the back of his hand. "No, we can't be friends. I want to be with you, Bess. It's agony being so close and not being able to be with you."

She nodded and hung her head. "When will I see you?"

He shrugged. "I dunno." His voice trembled.

"I'll write." Bess's eyes filled with tears again.

Nate sighed and gave her a single nod. "Thanks for the dance." He turned and hurried back into the dance hall. Without making eye contact with his friends, he stormed out into the darkness. He paused and punched out at the wall, severely bruising his knuckles. A sob escaped him and he took a deep breath and ran all the way back to his room in the boarding house.

Bess stood in the moonlight, deep sobs shook her body as she watched him leave. "Oh, Lord, if we aren't meant to be, help me to get over my feelings for him. This hurts so much." She shivered.

Frederick walked out and she hurriedly wiped at her cheeks.

"Are you alright, Bess? Did he hurt you?" Fred frowned.

"No, Nate would never hurt me. That is one thing I'm sure of." She sniffed back the tears again. "But I want to go home, please."

"Very well. I wasn't having a good time anyway. Mary Turkington is here, my old sweetheart, with my former best friend." He gritted his teeth. "Come on." He took her arm and led her from the dance hall out to the waiting carriage.

Henry frowned as he watched Nate storm out. He nudged Tim. They watched as Bess followed a few moments later with Fred. He could see she'd been crying. "What do you suppose happened?"

"Do you think she refused him again?"

"I'd say so by the look of death on his face." Henry grimaced.

* * * *

At last, in her own suite, Bess threw herself down on the bed and sobbed out her hurt and pain. "Lord, I'm in love with him; you know I am. Why can't I be with him? Why can't I have the man I love? Why do I have to sacrifice happiness and love?"

Didn't I sacrifice everything for you? I gave My Son's life for you. I know how it hurts my child, but I AM here. I have it all in my hand. Trust Me that I know what is best for you.

Bess heard the words deep in her heart, and she sat up abruptly and put her hands over her face, speaking her prayer aloud. "I'm sorry, Lord, you are right. You gave everything for me. Comparatively, this is nothing." She took a deep breath, pushed the feelings deep inside, and smiled a shaky smile. "I'll give You this, God. I'm willing to give up Nate, just like Abraham was willing to give up his son, and You gave up Yours. Your will be done, Lord. Help me with these feelings."

She fell to her knees, lifted her face to the heavens and began. "Our Father, who art in heaven, hallowed be Thy Name...."

Six

"Good morning, Dear?"

Bess sighed and took a seat at the dining table next to her aunt. "Morning." She nodded to Fred sitting opposite and gave him a sad smile.

Aunt Mere tilted her head. "How was the dance?"

Bess bit her lip to keep it from trembling.

"Mother, don't ask." Fred lifted a forkful of eggs into his mouth.

Meredith's eyes swung to her son. "Why? Did something happen?" She looked back at Bess. She had her head down and her hands in her lap.

"It's okay, Aunt Mere," she managed. "I'll be fine."

Aunt Mere nodded and changed the subject. Bess perked up somewhat, but a sadness hung over her.

No matter how hard Bess tried that day, she could not stop her mind from drifting to Nate, seeing herself whirling around the dancefloor in his arms. Each time she would have to wrestle with those thoughts and bring them back into line. *Lord, help me with these feelings. I know refusing Nate was the right thing to do, but I need Your help to take these feelings from me.*

* * * *

Nate stormed into the cafeteria and slumped into a chair. A darkness had hung over him that entire week, and he was constantly on the brink of tears. He'd barely uttered more than a few words to his friends.

"What's eating you?"

Nate looked up at Henry and shot him daggers. "Nothing."

Tim raised his brows. "That didn't sound very convincing. Something went down at the dance; your girl refused you again, didn't she?"

Nate closed his eyes. He sniffed back the tears that were so close to escaping. He gave his friends a single nod.

"I'm sorry, Chap." Henry grimaced at Tim.

Tim shrugged. "Well, at least now you know. You can move on."

Nate took a deep breath and exhaled. "I can't, Tim."

"Why not? There are plenty of lovely ladies in this city."

"Because I love her. I'll always love her. People don't turn off love so easily, not if it's true love." Nate's voice was low and resigned.

"Did she say why she doesn't love you?" Henry frowned.

Nate looked up. He managed a smirk. "That's the thing. She does love me. I know she does."

Tim tilted his head. "Hold on, you love her, and she loves you, yet she refused you? I don't understand. Did she say why?"

"Yes, she's told me several times." He shrugged.

"Care to share?" Henry waved over a waitress with the coffeepot and a tray of cups. She poured three cups and hurried away.

Nate paused and closed his eyes for a time. He took a deep breath and exhaled loudly. "She won't court because I'm not a Christian."

Henry and Tim raised their brows and looked at each other, took a sip of their coffee in unison, and put the cups down.

"Come again?" Henry scratched his chin.

Nate lifted sad, dark eyes to his friends. "She's a devout Christian. I admire that, her ability to believe in something so strongly." He sighed and flicked his hair off his face. "But she told me God is the most important person in her life, and she could never be with someone who didn't share that."

"But you wouldn't stop her going to church if she wanted to." Tim squinted and tilted his head.

"Course not." Nate shrugged. "I'd even go with her if she wanted me to." He took a long slurp of the hot liquid, it burnt his throat on the way down, but it was still less painful than the burning in his heart.

Henry shrugged. "So why don't you just tell her you're a Christian?"

Nate looked up. "Because she'd know if I don't mean it."

"And you don't?" Tim squinted at him.

Nate took a slurp and raised his brows in question.

Henry took over. "You don't believe in God?"

"I believe there is a God; I just don't think I can have the same faith she does. God's never done much for me. My parents are Christians too, but I just don't get it. Why would a supposed loving God let so many bad things happen to such a lovely girl like Bess?"

"What kind of things?" Henry drained his cup and clicked to the waitress for more.

"You may not have noticed because she was wearing gloves, but she has burn scars on her left hand and part way up her arm."

"What happened?" Tim asked as the waitress sloshed more black liquid in all three cups.

Nate took a breath and folded his arms across his chest. He leaned back and closed his eyes. "She lost her ma when she was six, and her pa died when she was nine. She ran the household for her older and younger brother, from that age, never got much of a childhood." He opened his eyes and his lips trembled.

His two friends listened carefully, nursing their coffee cups. They looked at Nate expectantly. He took a sip and continued. "When she was twelve, she and her younger brother were home alone; their older brother, was only fifteen, but was out getting an early start on the harvest. Bess was making breakfast and she left the room to fetch something. While she was out, her nine-year-old brother accidentally tripped over the rug while carrying a lantern. It smashed, and within seconds the curtains and house were on fire.

"A little wooden house like they had, was little more than kindling. It was in flames in no time. Their big brother saw the fire and came running, he managed to rescue Bess, but their younger brother was killed when the roof collapsed in. Left Bess with severe burns on her hand and arm. She spent weeks in the hospital in the city. She's fortunate to have the use of her left hand at all." Nate shook his head but then grinned. "She's the

51

toughest, bravest girl I know. There is not a drop of bitterness in her. I know that's because of her faith." His smile turned to a frown. "But I don't think I could honor a God that leaves a family to hurt like that. She's so faithful to God, and yet it seems He just heaps more and more hurt and pain on her.

"But the more pain heaped on her, the sweeter and kinder and more faithful she seems to become...." He sighed. "And it just makes me love her all the more." Nate closed his eyes and grimaced.

Tim and Henry said nothing for a time. They took several sips of their coffee.

"I'm sorry," Henry eventually managed. Tim nodded his agreement.

"I want to believe like she does. Trust me, I've wrestled with it this last week since the dance, trying to find if there was a way I could believe in God. But all I can think of is how angry I am at a God that would do that. I wish it were me that had suffered like that, not Bess."

"So what are you gonna do?" Tim scratched his chin.

Nate shrugged and grimaced. "Try to find a way to fall out of love with her, I suppose." He sighed loudly.

The two men nodded sadly; there were no words that would help their friend. They changed the subject back to their study in the hope that it would help Nate get over her.

*   *   *   *

"I'm sorry, Miss, I don't want to interrupt, but a note was left for you." The butler held an envelope out to her.

52

Bess looked up from her desk, put her pen down, and stood. "That's quite okay, Crews. I thank you for bringing it to me."

He nodded, backed out of her room and hurried down the hallway.

Bess turned it over and pulled out the small card. She read the printed words and tears flooded her eyes. She threw herself on her bed and sobbed as the words rang in her ears.

Bess, Thank you for the birthday greetings. I'm sorry, but I have to ask you not to write again. Somehow I have to find a way to forget about you.

Nate.

Bess spent more than an hour in prayer, longing to feel God's peace at the loss of a dear friend and the man she loved. It was worse than losing her father or even Joey, because Nate wasn't dead; he was still alive, and so close by. "Lord, I need You more than ever." She finished her prayer.

I AM with you. That voice in her soul spoke again. She sighed and nodded. "Yes, You are with me, Lord. I trust You with my broken heart. I trust that You will show me the way You wish me to go. Help me with my feelings, Lord."

At last, feeling a little more at peace, and determined to cling to God, she wiped her eyes and stood. She walked to her desk and picked up the pen, resuming her letter to Amber and to her brother.

* * * *

"Ohhhhh."

Aunt Meredith and Fred both lifted their heads to look at Bess.

"What is it, Dear?"

Bess lowered the letter into her lap, took a sip from her teacup, and smiled. "Sorry, I didn't mean to say that out loud."

"Did something happen?" Fred asked.

"Aaron rescued a woman and her child from a wagon wreck on our farm. Reading between the lines, it seems he's become quite fond of them." She smiled.

"Why do you say that?" Fred raised his brows. Aaron wasn't exactly the tenderest man.

Bess smiled as she lifted the letter again. "He was invited to spend Christmas with them. He told me he built the little girl a doll house with pegs for dolls." She lowered the letter again. "He made me one when I was a girl, with Pa's help. I remember the little painted faces on the peg people; I played with that dollhouse all the time." She sighed. "Till it burned up in the fire."

Aunt Meredith could see Bess's lip tremble. Ever since Nate's note, Bess had seemed to always be on the brink of tears. She bravely bore up under it, by clinging to God, but a broken heart doesn't mend quickly, nor does true love vanish easily.

The older woman reached across and squeezed Bess's hand and smiled kindly. Turning back to her own teacup, she took a sip. "Who is the woman?"

"Her name is Cass. Aaron told me in his last letter that she, her husband, and daughter were headed west to meet up with family at a new settlement. Wagon

54

trains sometimes cut through our farm. It would make Aaron so angry, all the mess they'd leave behind. Well, evidently something had delayed this family, the...." She skimmed the letter. "Harpers, and they were on their own. Somehow the wagon crashed down a hill. The woman and child were thrown from it and injured. Sadly the husband was killed. Aaron found them and brought them back to a neighbor's house.

"The little girl, Maisy, was uninjured; thank the Lord." Bess was full of genuine compassion for a child she'd never met. "The woman, Cass, is expecting her second child, and thankfully the baby is just fine. Cass broke her leg and severely bruised her ribs; she had lots of cuts and scrapes."

A wide smile crossed Bess's face then, and a sparkle entered her eye, one Meredith and Fred hadn't seen for a time. "Cass is up and about now, still uses a crutch, but Aaron says she's doing well. I'm reading between the lines here, and I think she's special to him. The little girl has definitely captured his heart. He's written...." She lifted the letter and counted the pages, "...three whole pages, double-sided, about Maisy."

"That sounds delightful. Do you think he loves her?" Aunt Meredith enjoyed Bess's newsy letters from home. It brought amusement and intrigue into her lonely life.

"I think he does." Bess grinned. "Although I don't think he realizes it yet." She closed her eyes. "Oh it would be so wonderful if it works out for them. He deserves happiness." A single tear trickled down her cheek.

"So do you, Bess." Fred looked over his newspaper.

"I know, and you are both so kind to care about me. I'm sorry I've been so somber, it's just... well, you know." She had shared with both all that had happened with Nate.

"We know, Dear. I had hoped Christmas might cheer you up some."

"I'm sorry I've been so low. But this..." She grinned and lifted the letter. "...gives me a reason to hope. Oh, I shall be praying for my brother. It's been a long time since he's had any happiness in his life."

"I'm glad, Dear. Maybe the New Year dance will cheer you up."

Bess screwed her nose up and shrugged. "I'm not so sure I want to go, Aunt Mere."

"Go on. You deserve to go out and have a good time."

Fred looked up. "You can come with Martha and I."

Bess smiled. "I'm so pleased you found Martha. I hope that works out for you."

Fred grimaced. "I'm not so sure we're compatible. We're just choosing to get to know each other." He fixed his eyes on his mother. "One thing for sure I will NOT marry a woman I do not love."

Meredith merely nodded, and coughed loudly.

Bess shuddered internally. Her aunt was getting weaker.

Seven

"Bess, there is someone here I'd like you to meet," Meredith called out when Bess returned from volunteering at an orphanage, as she did several times a week.

"Oh?" Bess walked into the drawing room. Her aunt looked very lively that day and had a grin on her face like a cat that had got the milk. It was a relief. The woman had been low for some time, and Bess knew she didn't have many weeks left.

A gentleman stood as she entered. Aunt Mere remained seated. Fred looked over his paper and gave Bess a sympathetic look, as though he was apologizing for his mother's actions.

"Bess, Dear, this is Milton Theodore Alexander Nelson the third, of the East Street Nelsons. His father is a cousin of my late husband. He's from a good family, and he's heir to his father's fortune and import-export company."

Bess nodded and turned to look at the man. She knew his credentials were supposed to impress her, but she preferred to get to know a person based on their character, not their bank balance. She smiled at the man politely, quickly sizing him up. He was tall, at least head and shoulders taller than her, thin and a little gaunt. He had slicked-back blond hair and rather dull blue eyes. He looked to be like most in that set; she was getting used to people like this.

The awkward silence was deafening. Aunt Mere's grin grew. "Milt, this is my niece, Elizabeth Rose Carter."

The man stepped towards her and put his hand out, took hers, and lifted it to his lips. "A pleasure to meet you, Miss Carter."

Bess looked horrified and snatched back her hand. She stepped back from him.

"He's here to escort you to the New Year's Eve Dance this evening." Aunt Meredith looked delighted.

"Ohhhhh." Bess hadn't meant to gasp so loudly. Her eyes grew wide. "Oh, Aunty, that's not necessary, I'm not even certain I want to go."

"Now, Bess, Milt is a cousin, and he's come especially to escort you to the dance tonight. I hope you'll allow him to accompany you and have a wonderful time with him. Please, Dear, it'd make an old woman very happy."

Bess seethed internally; it wasn't fair for her aunt to put her in this position. She could hardly refuse with the man standing there. She blinked back threatening tears and swallowed rapidly.

"Allow me." Milton stepped forward. He retook Bess's hand and rested his other on top. She looked up at him. "Miss Carter, I would very much enjoy being your escort for the evening if you will allow me. I have the most honorable of intentions. I shall take you to the dance, and escort you home, and you will be quite safe with me, I can assure you."

"I.... Ummm... I'm sorry, this has just caught me off guard."

"Well, will you?" Meredith's face was so bright with joy, Bess couldn't refuse her.

"Very well. I will just go dress." She smiled kindly at the man.

"Take your time, Miss Carter. Knowles will come for us in an hour." The young man touched her arm gently.

Bess nodded and hurried away. She shut her bedroom door forcefully and leaned back against it. With her eyes closed, she sighed loudly. If there was one thing she really didn't like, it was matchmakers. That was always up to the Lord, not other people. She was not interested in courting a random man that her aunt picked out. Still, her aunt didn't have much longer to live, and this would make her happy. She didn't have to court the man, just go to a dance with him. Besides, Fred would be there too.

"Oh, Miss Carter. You are truly elegant." The man eyed her up and down as she walked down the stairs in her new pale pink silk gown, and long ivory gloves. Agatha had done her hair, which was very becoming and made her look a lot older than her seventeen years.

"Thank you, Mr. Nelson." She smiled kindly and took the hand he reached out to help her down the last few stairs. It was the polite thing to do. *I managed to walk down the other twenty-eight stairs on my own, but the last two I needed help with.* She chuckled internally.

She looked up at him, her eyes steely. "Let me say one thing, before we go."

"I'm listening, Miss Carter."

"I want you to know, this is not a courtship."

He smiled. "Of course not; we are simply going to a dance." He lifted his arm to her, and they walked towards the door together. "What happens after that remains to be seen," he murmured under his breath.

"What was that?"

He walked her out to the carriage where Fred and Martha were already waiting. "Oh, I just said, I understand, and I hope we just have a nice evening."

*   *   *   *

The dance was, as they always were, stuffy and formal. Milton was a gentleman and treated Bess kindly, bringing her drinks and leading her in waltzes and reels. She warmed up to him somewhat over the night. Friends? No, but he was no longer a complete stranger. Bess found him dull and uninteresting most of the time. He talked about business non-stop and never stopped to learn anything about her.

She found out he was thirty-three years old and, by his own reckoning, about the most eligible bachelor in town. "You know I could have any of the women here. They constantly fawn over me. I'm very wealthy," he announced as they took up the final dance.

"Why didn't you invite one of them to the dance?" Bess asked, not unkindly, but she wasn't impressed by his snobbery.

"Because your aunt asked me to accompany you. I was happy to oblige, and now that I know you, I'm glad I did." He grinned. "It's always good for a man's reputation to have a lovely young thing on his arm."

Bess raised her brows. "Thing?"

He smiled his apology. "I just mean a beautiful girl like you makes me look good. Besides, you're charming company. I should like to take you out again sometime."

Bess said nothing. She dropped his arms as the dance finished, and allowed herself to be led around while he farewelled his chums, making sure to touch her just as often as he could. It was a little too familiar for an acquaintance, but still, Bess said nothing. He'd not done anything improper; she just hoped he wasn't getting the wrong idea.

At last, they walked out of the wide foyer of the building and onto the street to wait for the carriage. Just at that moment, a man strode around the corner, somewhat intoxicated. Milton leaped out of the way so he didn't get hit. The man crashed right into Bess, knocking her to the ground.

Milt leaped forward, without bothering to help Bess up. "Watch where you're going, you buffoon."

Bess made her way to her feet, frowned at both men, and brushed the dirt off her gown, grimacing at the long streaks of mud that now covered it. Milton noticed Bess and stepped beside her, placing his hand on her back. "You alright, Darling?"

Bess raised her brows at him.

"Oh, well, excuuuuse me, Mr. toffee nose," the man sneered.

Bess's head snapped up and her mouth dropped. She'd recognize that voice anywhere, even when slightly slurred. "Nate?"

"Bess?" Nate squinted at her. Milton, threatened that his trophy was going to leave him, put his arm around her waist and pulled her close to him.

Nate caught the gesture, but not the grimace on her face. He nodded and sneered. "Oh, I see how it is. Good evening. Don't let me interrupt your date." His voice evidenced his hurt.

"We're not on a...." Bess began to protest, but Milton shut her down.

"No, that's fine, no harm done. Just be more careful next time. You almost knocked me down." Milton thrust a hand out to him.

Nate grimaced. *She turned me down for this snob, he doesn't give a fig about her.* He sighed, and he couldn't help but notice how beautiful, how radiant she was, even with the streaks of mud on her clothing and the smallest smudge on her cheek. It was oddly endearing, and his heart began to bleed. He nodded and looked her in the eye.

Bess ached. She could see the deep hurt on his face.

"Good evening." He gave her a sad smile and turned to hurry away.

Bess stepped forward. "Nate," she called after him. He paused for a moment, sighed, and kept walking.

"Nate, please don't go. It's not what it seems," she called after him.

Milton grabbed her by the waist and pulled her back. "Don't waste your time on him, Miss Carter." He squeezed her arm tightly and leaned in. His voice became stern. "Come now, my dear, do be charming and don't yell out to drunks on the street. Do you know how that makes me look?"

Bess frowned and stepped away from him. "Mr. Nelson, I will call out to whom I please. You have no say over my behavior, whatsoever! Now won't you please take me home?"

Fred arrived with the carriage; he opened the door and jumped out. She raised her brows to him, pleading for help. He got the message.

"We must hurry, Bess. Knowles is anxious to get the carriage back. He must rest the horses, and I need him to take me to the cottage tomorrow to see to the repairs. We mean to get an early start."

Bess flashed him a grateful smile and took his offered hand up into the carriage where Martha was waiting. Fred turned to Milton. "Thank you, Milt. I'll see to it the ladies get home."

"But I was to escort her home."

"That's quite okay. I'll escort her. I'm happy to, It'll save you the detour." Fred leaped up onto the carriage, and called out, "Home, Knowles." He closed the door abruptly.

Knowles clucked to the horses and was off before Milton could protest.

"Thank you." Bess's face held deep gratefulness, and she explained what had happened.

Fred nodded and took his seat next to Martha. Seeing Bess hang her head and sigh, he reached across to touch her arm. "I'm sorry about Nate."

"Thank you," she whispered. All the carefully hidden feelings came swirling up inside her, and she swallowed rapidly in a futile attempt to hold back the tears. Failing, she lifted her handkerchief to her eyes.

Fred squeezed her hand again, and she gave him a slow smile.

*   *   *   *

Nate hurried around the corner and into the nearest saloon. He slumped onto a stool and thumped the bar. "Whiskey."

"Coming, no need to yell." The bartender reached for a bottle and a glass, walked over to him, and slopped some into the glass.

Nate swigged it down in one go, thrust the glass down, and gestured for more. The bartender frowned but poured more in. Nate swigged that one back, too, and leaned forward with his elbows on the bar. The burning whiskey did nothing to quench his already burning soul. *She moved on awfully quick. I guess it takes someone a lot wealthier than me to make her change her tune.* He sighed again and nodded. *At least I know that door is closed, slammed tightly shut.* Nate stayed in his spot until the clock issued in the new year. Somehow he managed to slither home to the boarding house.

*   *   *   *

Bess didn't leave her suite for two days. She spent a lot of that time on her knees, petitioning the Lord to take the ache from her heart. No matter how much she'd tried and pleaded with God, she couldn't stop loving Nate. Seeing him that night with such hurt in his eyes trampled her already broken heart into more pieces. *I know that hurt is because of me. I still know I did the right thing; I could never court an unbeliever. Oh, Lord. Please heal Nate's heart. He doesn't deserve the hurt either. Please show me Your plan for my life and help me to get over him.*

"Agatha, has Bess come down?" Meredith called the maid as she passed in the hall.

Agatha walked into the drawing room and stood before her. "No, Ma'am, she still won't come out. She's been weeping a lot."

Aunt Meredith grimaced. "Alright, thank you, Agatha."

"Ma'am, shall I get the cook to prepare a tray for her and take it up?"

"Yes, thank you, Agatha. That would be most kind. Perhaps she'll eat something at least."

But Bess only picked at the food. She slumped down on the bed and sighed. Somehow she had to pick herself up and carry on. Nate was her past, and she had to get over him; somehow. "No more wallowing in self-pity," she determined. "Lord, I am Your servant, and I will follow You, even if I do it alone." She forced back the threatening tears and stood up.

"Have I not commanded thee? Be strong and of a good courage; be not afraid, neither be thou dismayed: for the Lord thy God is with thee whithersoever thou goest." Bess quoted, three times to herself. She felt the peace of the Lord wash over her. It didn't take away the pain but gave her the strength to carry on. "Yes, You are with me whithersoever I go. Thank You, Lord, for sustaining me. Please take care of Nate. I don't want to see him hurting." She smiled, gave herself a nod in the mirror, and hurried out to join her family for supper.

"I am so sorry, Dear. I should never have made you go with Milton." Meredith gave Bess a sad smile as the girl took the chair opposite her.

"No, Aunty, it's not your fault. Milton was a gentleman; he just already had a first love."

Both Meredith and Fred put down their forks and frowned.

Bess chuckled, wiped her mouth on her napkin, and grinned. "Himself. I know he's your cousin, and he's very connected, Aunt Merc. I won't be unkind, but he seemed rather... preoccupied with his own image, rather than me. But that's not why I've been upset. I've dealt with the likes of Milt before."

"Then what was it?"

Fred answered on her behalf. "I told you, Mother, she ran into Nate. Or he ran into her."

"Yes." Bess gave her aunt a sad smile. "I believe he thought I was courting Milton. I could tell by the hurt in his eyes."

Aunt Mere sipped her tea. "And there really is no future for the two of you?"

Bess shrugged. "I love him, I think I always will, but I cannot and will not betray my God. He's made it clear in Scripture to not be joined with unbelievers, not in something so important as whom I spend my life with. I'd rather be a spinster than not be able to share the joy of the Lord with the man I marry." Her voice was determined, but both mother and son could see the quiver to her lips.

Meredith squinted. "I don't understand why you would put yourself through this and not allow yourself to love."

Bess didn't hesitate. "I would lay down my life for my God, Aunt Mere." She blinked away a tear. "This sacrifice is the least I can do for the Lord; after all He's done for me. If He allows me to find the love of a godly, wonderful man, then so be it. But I won't defy Him just to make myself happy."

Meredith and Fred smiled. "I'm impressed by your faith, Bess."

"Thank you, Fred. You could have a faith like that too."

He merely nodded, and the three ate their supper in silence.

Eight

"I've never seen you so determined, Sawyer."

Nate shrugged and looked up from his book. "Yeah, well, love didn't work out for me. At least I can try to get my law degree; gotta have something to live for."

"I admire that." Henry scratched his chin. "But you need to take a break sometime. Can't you just sit in the cafeteria and enjoy your meal? You don't have to study twenty-four hours a day."

Nate looked up and sighed. "If I let my brain stop, I'll dwell on what I've lost...." Another sigh. "So I have to keep it busy. It's bad enough that she haunts my dreams...!" An even louder sigh.

"Fair enough. But you'll at least take Spring Break off, won't you?" Tim slumped into the chair next to Henry, three cups of coffee in his hand. He slid one across to Nate, and Henry snatched the other one.

Nate closed the book, swallowed back his feelings, and grinned. "What do you have in mind, chaps?"

Henry and Tim raised their brows at each other. "Well, nothing yet." Tim scratched his chin. "But I'm sure we can come up with something."

"So, Sawyer, are you gonna move into my father's house or not? He's looking for some clerks too. We can both work for him."

"Yeah, I think I will. I do need to earn some money. My savings are running low." He grimaced. *I spent far too much on whiskey trying to drown my sorrows.*

"Well, Father says you can stay rent-free, provided you give him ten to fifteen hours a week, around studies and work full time over summer."

Nate frowned. "What would I have to do?"

"We'd both be clerks, paperwork, filing, taking and sorting orders. Pays a dollar a week, part-time, double when full-time."

Nate scratched his chin. "Yeah, that sounds good. That's good money and it'll provide a good distraction. Alright, count me in. I'll move in over Spring Break."

Henry grinned. "Excellent, that's great news."

*　*　*　*

Bess put her hand on the woman's shoulder and bent down to kiss her forehead. "Goodbye, Aunt Meredith. I love you." She wiped a tear away as she stepped back.

Fred put his arm around Bess, and she leaned her head against his shoulder.

The doctor pulled the sheet up over the woman while the reverend in the corner prayed aloud, holding his Bible open in front of him.

"I'm so sorry, Fred."

Fred put his other arm across her and squeezed Bess slightly. "Thank you, Cousin. I'm glad she's not sick anymore."

"Me too. I'm so glad I came and spent these months with her. I love her so much. I feel like I've got to know my mother."

They left the room together. They needed to meet with the undertaker and the pastor to arrange the funeral. While they waited in the drawing room, Fred had Agatha bring them tea.

"Bess."

She put her tea cup down and looked up at Fred. "Yes?"

"You won't go home right away, will you?"

Bess shrugged. "I'm not sure what I'll do. I don't know what to do about the cottage, or where I'm supposed to be right now. I did promise I would stay until we have it all settled."

"Good, I don't think I could handle all this without you. You're a wise girl."

"Fred, I'm not yet eighteen, and you're in your mid-twenties. You have much more experience than I do."

"Yes, but you have a sensible, practical, and mature head on your shoulders. You aren't manipulated or enamored by wealth, and, I could really use that."

"Well, I'll stay as long as you need me to, Cousin."

"So when you go home for your brother's wedding, you'll come back?"

"Yes, my brother's wedding is in August, and Amber's is a week later. I'll stay a few weeks and then come back."

Fred reached over and gripped her hand. "I appreciate that. You know my mother really loved you. She told me a few days ago that she felt like her sister was back in her life. She hopes you'll keep the cottage and use it, maybe even live there long-term?"

Bess smiled. "Thank you. I really loved her too. You know, Aaron falsely judged you all these years. He thought you were snobbish and condescending, sending all those checks."

"I didn't mean it to sound like that. We've thought about you both often, and Mother wanted to help. She loved your mother dearly, and she just wanted to do what she could for her precious Lu's children. I guess we didn't see how it would come across. Truthfully, I respect Aaron for keeping you together all those years. I don't know if I could have been as tough at twelve-years-old to take over a farm and raise two siblings."

Bess brushed a tear off her cheek. "Which is why I'm thrilled for him and Cass. He's worked so hard."

"It's a shame he never got to go to Medical School like he wanted."

"Yeah. I guess life changes, and we don't always get what we want." She sighed.

Fred squeezed her hand. "I'm sorry about you and Nate. I know it's still really hard for you. And it's your birthday in a few weeks, and you'd have liked him to be there."

"Thank you, Fred. You've been so understanding. Yes. I had hoped things would work out with Nate." She shrugged. "I haven't heard anything from him since I bumped into him at New Year's Eve. It's been what, five months?"

He nodded. "And you still haven't got over him?"

Bess gave him a sad smile. "I don't suppose I ever will. I guess that's why I turned Matthais down last week, when he came calling. He's a lovely, Christian man, and I like him well enough, but deep down inside, my heart belongs to Nate. Until that changes, it wouldn't be fair to any other man. I still hold out hope that one day Nate will come to the Lord."

"Do you think if that happens, he'll still want to be with you?"

Bess shrugged and sighed. "I'm not sure. I'm not expecting or demanding anything to happen. It's all up to God. I trust Him to know best. I've prayed and prayed that He'll help me with my feelings, but I just end up loving Nate all the more. Perhaps in the future, we are supposed to be together, and God is ensuring I won't give my heart to anyone else."

"Bess, are you sure you aren't setting yourself up for a life of loneliness?"

"No, I'm not afraid to be alone. I have the Lord. I know God. He cares about me and is always with me. And if He wants me to love another man, He'll take these feelings for Nate from me. That wouldn't be fair to any man."

"Good for you. I couldn't marry someone who didn't love me with all their heart, and I didn't love with all my heart."

Bess smiled. "I pray every day that it'll happen for you, Cousin. You deserve to be happy."

"Thank you, Bess." They both stood as the pastor and undertaker entered the room.

*   *   *   *

"So, how much money have you saved?"

"That's not your business, Henry Martin. My money is my own." Nate chuckled. "Seriously, about twelve dollars, I think, after I've purchased a few things."

"How much are you aiming for?"

Nate grimaced. "Enough for law school next year, and then to sit the bar."

"Oh, you'll be happy to get more hours work for Father then."

"Yeah, I'm managing twenty hours around study okay. It's a challenge, and you know I seldom get out these days. But it'll be worth it when I'm a lawyer."

"Sawyer the Lawyer," Henry mocked.

Nate smirked. "The irony hasn't escaped me. However, I hope to be Sawyer the Attorney in time."

"And you really plan to go back to that tiny little town you grew up in?" Henry screwed his face up.

Nate nodded. "If not there, then somewhere similar."

"The prairies?" Henry put down his cup and leaned back on the chaise, it was the least comfortable chair in the living room, but he'd always loved it.

"Yes, the prairies. I'm a farm boy, remember."

"Yeah, but you'll be a lawyer, an attorney. You could get a practice in the city, Chicago, New York, Boston, anywhere."

"I'm sorry, but you can't convince me. I've enjoyed being in the city to a point, but only because I know it's temporary. I've got prairie in my blood. Besides, they are so under-represented legally out there."

"You won't make nearly as much as you could in the city."

"I know that. I imagine many of my clients won't be able to pay, least not in cash."

"What else can you pay with?"

Nate grinned. "Chickens, canned apples, a big case might earn a prized hog."

Henry laughed so hard he spilled tea on the rug. He grimaced and pulled the cord for Herman, their butler.

"Well, I suppose we better get back to our books. Gotta work at the factory this afternoon."

Both men drained their cups. Herman cleaned the spill and took their cups while the scholars hurried to their rooms to study.

*   *   *   *

"Knowles is headed this way, Sir."

Fred grinned and patted the butler's shoulder. "Thank you, Crews. Is everything ready?"

"Yes, Sir, the drawing room is all set up. We are just waiting for you and the guest of honor. The other guests are assembled and waiting."

"Very good, I best get out there. Thanks for doing this for her."

"Least we can do, Sir. We all think very highly of Miss Bess."

"I know you do, Crews, and I appreciate that." He nodded and headed out to the carriage. Knowles was just opening the door and helping Bess down.

She stepped onto the cobblestoned path and looked up at her cousin. He didn't usually come to greet her. "Is everything okay?"

"Yes, I just came to welcome you home."

Bess squinted at him. "What are you up to?"

Fred shrugged. "I'm not up to anything. Would you allow me?" He offered her his arm.

She grinned as she took it and he led her towards the wide foyer. "Something fishy is going on here. You're acting strange."

Fred grinned but said nothing. He turned toward the drawing room.

Bess tipped her head to the side. "Where are we going?"

"You'll see."

Crews stood outside the closed doors of the drawing room. Bess frowned; they were almost never closed unless an important meeting was taking place.

At Fred's nod, Crews opened the doors and Bess gasped, leaping in fright as the gathered group called out, "Happy Birthday!"

"Ohhhh." Bess's eyes flooded with tears as she took a step inside. She looked around. Flowers and ribbons adorned the room, and long tables held food. The entire household staff was lined up along one side. At least twenty people stood around with glasses in hand.

"For she's a jolly good fellow...." One person began to sing, and the entire crowd joined in.

Bess stood with tears in her eyes until they finished. "Thank you. Oh, this was so unnecessary."

"Bess, you only turn eighteen once, and you've been such a help to me. You deserve this. I know you're going home in a few weeks for your brother's wedding, and I want to tell you how much you mean to me. And to try to encourage you to come back."

Bess wiped her eyes and stood to kiss her cousin on the cheek. "Thank you, Cousin. And yes, I will come back. I promised you I would."

"Now, let's get on with the celebration."

Bess grinned and walked around to greet everyone, people she'd befriended at church and some of those she'd met at events. "Thank you all for coming," she said. "Please, eat up." They all laughed, and the festivities began.

*   *   *   *

"Why the long face?"

Nate slumped into his chair at the cafeteria and slapped his satchel down on the table. He scowled at Tim. "It's June twenty-sixth." He shrugged.

Henry swallowed, his mouthful of muffin and raised his brows. "So?"

Nate nodded his thanks to the waitress who placed a cup of black coffee before him. He rested his head on his hand, leaning on his elbow, he sighed again. "Bess's birthday; she's turning eighteen today."

Tim rolled his eyes. "Have you still not gotten over her?"

"I love her, Tim, always will, I guess." He grimaced.

"I thought maybe lovely Amelia might cure you of that." Tim raised his brows suggestively.

Nate frowned. "Amelia was nice enough, a little snobby, I guess, and she's pretty, but..." he sighed again.

"She's not Bess," Henry and Tim said at the same time.

Nate closed his eyes and shook his head slowly. "No matter how hard I try, I just can't fall out of love with her. It's agonizing."

"What do you suppose she's doing?" Henry slurped at his coffee.

"Probably getting engaged to that fella I saw her with. There's no way Bess would stay unattached for long. She's so lovely, someone will snap her up. Someone smarter than me."

"Are you sure? There's always a chance, isn't there?" Henry drained his cup.

Nate shrugged. "She's made her position clear. I don't think I'll get another chance with her. I have to let her go. I just don't seem to be able to. I tried silencing it with whiskey, but that failed as I knew it would. I've thrown myself into study and work, but still, whenever I close my eyes, I see Bess floating into that cotillion in that green dress, looking like an angel." He sighed again and ran his fingers through his hair. "Then I see her with him."

"Doesn't mean she's still with him." Tim shrugged. "And even so, there is another way to drown your sorrows, that's sure to get your mind off that trollop."

Nate sat up, glared at Tim and gritted his teeth. "Don't you ever call her that again. You may be my friend, but I will knock you into next week if you ever insult her again."

Tim leaned back. "Okay, alright, back down, Nate. You're awfully protective of a woman who rejected you."

"Doesn't mean I don't still love her. When love is true and honest, it doesn't just switch off. I'm not sure I'll ever stop loving her, even if I can never be with her."

"You sure have it bad, Sawyer!" Tim shook his head. "I just don't get it; I fall in and out of love every day." He raised his brows and made a kissing gesture to a young lady nearby. The woman shuddered and hurried away.

"Then it's not love, Tim. If you really loved a woman, you'd never be able to even consider another woman."

"You country boys are so quaint. I thought we'd finally beaten the prairie outta you." Tim drained his cup.

"Nope, sorry. Still just a country boy." Nate managed a sideways smile.

"Well, come on, chaps, let's go find a way to help Nate get his mind off Bess."

"What are you planning?" Nate squinted at Henry.

"We'll work it out as we go. Anything is better than sitting here watching you wallow in your self-pity." Tim grimaced.

Nate nodded, drained his cup, and stood to follow his friends out.

*   *   *   *

"Good morning, Cousin." Bess sat down at the breakfast table.

"Good morning."

Bess smiled her thank you to Agatha as she placed a bowl of oatmeal before her. "Thank you for last night. It was such a lovely surprise."

"It's my pleasure, Bess. You deserve it. You've worked hard for the estate, and you've been volunteering at the church and the orphanage."

"I know, I've been so busy. It was nice to have a night to forget that. It was lovely to not have young men with ulterior motives floating around. And thank you for not inviting your cousin Milton."

Fred rolled his eyes. "Oh, I can't abide Milt. He may be a cousin, but he's a frightful bore and way too familiar with young women."

"I know. I'm glad I only spent one evening with him. I was taught not to speak unkindly of people, but, something about him made my skin crawl. I can't place my finger on it, but he was very possessive. I felt like I was only there to make him look good."

"There is a reason he's thirty-eight and single."

"Thirty-eight? He told me he was thirty-three." She shuddered. "He's old enough to be my father."

"That's why I never took my eyes off you. I know what he's like. I couldn't believe Mother foisted him on you in the first place."

"It's okay; she meant well."

Fred smiled and shook his head. "You really do see the best in everyone, don't you?"

Bess shrugged. "I've always tried to. I'm far from perfect, but I've been forgiven much by the Lord, and I think others deserve forgiveness from me. All people have the capability to do good things and bad things. 'There but for the grace of God go I.' I believe that. I have to choose to make the decisions that honor God."

"Like with Nate."

"Yes." She sighed. "I can't solely live to please myself and treat people as pawns to further my ambitions. Scripture says the first shall be last and the last first. Christ was my example as a servant, and the way He loved people, even the worst of sinners like me, is truly inspirational. I fall way short of His standards, but with His help, I do my utmost. It breaks my heart to hurt Nate so." Her lips trembled. "Seeing the pain in his eyes will always haunt me, especially knowing it was me who put it there." She hung her head. "But I have to be true to my God. That doesn't mean things will always be easy."

"Bess, you are an inspiration to me in my fledgling faith. Thank you for introducing me to a loving God."

Bess's face lit up. "Oh, I'm so thrilled you've given your heart to Christ, Fred. Any lost sheep who comes back to the fold is a reason to rejoice. I'm beyond delighted for my brother. If only my best friend Amber would take her faith more seriously and...."

"And?" Fred raised his brows.

She gave him a shy smile.

He nodded. "And Nate?"

"Yes, but I can't force either of them to submit to God. It's gotta come from the heart."

"I love the way you truly love people and care for their souls."

Bess shuddered. "I can't bear the thought of the people I love, or any people for that matter, not being in heaven. The alternative is unthinkable. I really don't want that for anyone."

Fred reached across and squeezed her hand. "I'm gonna miss you when you go home."

"I'm coming back, Fred. I promised I'd stay with you for a time."

Fred grimaced. "Then you'll leave me to go back for good, unless I can convince you to move into your cottage full-time."

"I could for a time, but my heart will always be on the prairie. Robertson Township is my home. All the people I love live there, save you and...."

"And Nate?"

"Yeah, and being in this town, knowing he's here, is so hard. I know where he lives, and I just wanna go there and throw myself in his arms."

"Well, for what it's worth, when you do finally go home for good. I'll miss you."

"We're only a letter away from each other, Cousin."

Fred looked up as the butler entered the room with the post. "Speaking of letters." He smiled and nodded his thanks to Crews as he lifted the four envelopes off the tray. "Thank you, Crews."

"Sir." The butler bowed slightly and left the room.

Bess chuckled. "He's much too serious for his own good."

"That's Crews' way. He's been butler in this house since he was twenty-two. He takes his job very seriously. Hey, this one's for you?"

Bess reached for it and turned it over. "Cass." She grinned. "I'm so thrilled she had the gumption to write to me. I'm enjoying getting to know her by post. She'll be my sister-in-law soon, and her children will be my niece and nephew. I can't wait." She put her thumb under the envelope and slid out the letter.

Perusing it, she grinned and put her hand to her mouth. She gasped as an idea sprung to mind.

Fred looked up from his own letter. "Is everything okay?"

"Yes. Oh, I wonder, is it possible?"

"Is what possible?"

"Well, let me read this to you."

Don't mention this to Aaron, but we've been talking about him being a doctor one day. Bess, he's so gifted. Even with the little knowledge he has from reading and studying, he is calm and clever. He put me so at ease when he rescued me, and when he delivered Henry. He needs to be a doctor. It saddens me that he's given up on that dream. But we simply can't afford to move to the city to train.

I've been praying about it, but there doesn't seem to be any way around it. Even with our savings combined, it's not nearly enough for rent in the city, and college tuition, not to mention two small children to care for. I'm sad for him. He would make the most wonderful doctor. And I'm not just biased; Tam and Connie agree with me. But even if the entire town were to chip in, we'd still not have nearly enough money.

Fred nodded. "What are you thinking?"

"I can't do much about getting him into college, but if he could get in, they could live in the cottage. There is plenty of room, and it's just a short walk to campus. They'd not need to pay a cent; we own it outright. It's rightfully half his anyway. Oh, do you think it's possible?"

Fred stroked his chin. "Leave it to me, Bess. I've got some contacts at the college. I'll see what I can do."

* * * *

"I'm really going to miss you, Cousin. Please don't stay there and never come back." Fred embraced Bess.

Bess picked up her carpet bag and grinned. "I'll be back before September, hopefully with Aaron and his family in tow. Cass is convinced he'll say yes."

"I want to say I hope so, but I guess you'll move into the cottage with them?"

Bess grinned. "I've been thinking about that, and, a newly married couple deserves their privacy. He has a family to think of. I think I'll leave them to the cottage...."

"And stay here with me?"

"For now."

"Oh, Bess, that's the best news. I've come to rely on you."

"No pressure. Now are you sure you can cope for a few weeks without me?"

He grimaced. "Crews will keep me in line, and I better get used to it. One day you'll leave me, and I'll be all alone."

"There will be a future Mrs. Bennett, lady of the manor. I know it, and I feel like it'll be sooner rather than later."

The conductor's voice cut her off. She squeezed his arm, kissed his cheek, and hurried onto the train. Standing on the steps, she waved. "See you in a month."

"See you." He waved back, then turned to meet Knowles in the carriage.

* * * *

"Good to have the year finished, Chaps. Only one more to go." Henry slapped his friends on the back. "Let me take you both out to celebrate your exam results. We all did well."

"Not as well as the country boy. Where'd you pull that out of?" Tim grimaced and thrust his finger at Nate's paper. "Ninety-three percent average. Who knew country boys were so clever?"

Nate grimaced. "It helps when you are trying to distract your mind, I guess. You chaps did well too."

"I only got eighty-seven, and the ladies' man over here, just scraped into the seventies."

Tim chuckled. "Other priorities, I guess." He winked at a woman walking past them up the street.

Nate shook his head. "Do you ever actually have any success with the ladies with your methods?"

"More success than you," Tim scoffed.

Nate sighed. "Low blow!"

"Sorry, I didn't mean that."

Nate grimaced and shook his head. "Yeah, you did. I guess you're right. We're both as pathetic as each other."

Henry changed the subject. "Well, chaps, tonight we party big. The food and drinks are on me." He flashed them a sideways smile. "At least on my father."

Nate grimaced. "We can't go too big, you and I have to work tomorrow, remember? Your father only gave us one day off."

"Oh, we'll be fine. Stop being such a country boy. Let your hair down; let's have some fun."

Nate grinned at Henry. "Okay." He thrust his examination results into his pocket and hurried off after his pals.

Nine

"Oh, Aaron, I can't believe today is finally your wedding day. I'm beyond thrilled for you."

Aaron embraced Bess and kissed her hair. "Thank you, Sister. Life has never looked brighter."

A tear ran down her cheek and Aaron brushed it off. "Hey, what is it? Is it Nate?"

She sighed. "Yeah, there's a little of 'what might have been,' but that's not what I'm thinking. These are happy tears. I've been praying for you for so long, and God has answered my prayers. I get to see you happy, with a family of your own, and you get to live your dream of being a doctor. I couldn't be more thrilled for you."

Aaron embraced her again. "Thanks to Cousin Frederick getting me that scholarship and you for letting me stay in your house."

Bess pulled back. "Hey, it's as much yours as it is mine. The inheritance is for both of us, and it's more than I could ever spend in a lifetime."

"Nah, it's all yours, Sister. I don't want for anything. I'm beyond grateful that you're allowing me to live there, but after that, I don't need it. Just having that woman by my side and those two incredible children... That's all the blessing I need."

Bess bit her lips together nervously. She stepped back and put her hands behind her back, rocking on her feet, trying to look innocent.

Aaron squinted. "I know that look, Bess Carter. What are you hiding?"

"I did something."

He raised his brows and crossed his arms over his new suit.

"I bought a building."

Aaron frowned. "You did? A house are you going to move back here?"

Bess smiled. "No, it's not a house, well, it is a house, but it's not for me."

"What are you saying?"

"Aaron, please don't be mad. I purchased the old boarding house in town. I've arranged to convert the upstairs into a lovely home, and the downstairs...."

Aaron glared at her. "The downstairs?"

"The downstairs into a clinic and recovery rooms."

"A clinic, what are you saying?"

"For you, silly, when you come back as Doctor Aaron Carter. You can live upstairs and work downstairs."

"But what about the farm?"

"Aaron, you will be too busy with your family and your clinic to farm. Sell it to Amber and Vincent, when you get back."

Aaron scratched his chin and walked away from her. She looked down and sighed. *Great, you went too far splashing around your money, Bess Carter!*

She heard her brother sigh loudly. He turned and lunged at her, wrapping her in a tight bear hug. "Thank you. You've been so kind to me all these years, and now this. I can never repay you. Of course I can't farm if I'm a doctor. You have it all worked out."

Bess stepped back from him and wiped at her tears. "Aaron, all I ever wanted was for you to be happy. You have sacrificed everything to give me a good life, and this doesn't come close to repaying all you've done for me. You put aside your own healing and hurts to help me through. You never need to feel like you owe me. This is just the very least I can do. I love you so very much, Brother." She glanced at the clock. "Oh, we'd better go. We can't have the groom being late for his own wedding."

They hurried out. "Thanks for everything, Sister. And for being willing to move into the little apartment while you are here, to look after the children so we can have a honeymoon. I'll miss you though."

"No you won't; you'll have your new wife with you." Her eyes sparkled in genuine joy.

Aaron helped her up onto the gig, careful not to snag her new dress.

"Wife." He grinned as he leaped up and flicked the reins. "Who'd have thought it?"

"You deserve this happiness. I'm thrilled to stay in the little apartment and look after my new little niece and nephew for a week. They are dear children."

He winked at her and clucked to Snowflake, trying to get more speed out of her. "Shoulda hitched it to Flash, we'd make it in record time."

"Oh? Anxious are we?"

Aaron rolled his eyes. "Beyond anxious. I was ready to marry that woman months ago."

"By the way, Happy Birthday, Big Brother."

Aaron squeezed the hand that lay on his arm. "Thank you. It's still a little bittersweet to hear that. It's still the day our father died." He sighed but then smiled. "But I feel like I've redeemed this day forever. I can remember Pa and celebrate my anniversary and birthday all in one day."

"I'm so glad. I've been dying to say those two words to you for years."

Aaron squeezed his sister's arm. "Thank you."

"Consider the clinic a birthday present." She nodded towards the building, now boarded up. A sign outside said, 'Under Construction.' "It'll be ready for you, when you get back, Doctor. This town will be so blessed to have you."

"Huh, never thought I'd hear that. They all hated me for so long."

"They didn't hate you; they just didn't understand."

Aaron pulled the gig to a stop. Mr. Archer stepped forward to take it from him. Aaron nodded to the man and embraced his sister. He strode in to take his place at the front. Bess stood outside to await the bride.

* * * *

"This isn't much of a house."

"Amber, it's all I need for now. It's just me and the children for a week." Bess slumped down on the couch and sighed. "It was such a beautiful wedding."

"Yes, I never thought I'd see the day! Your brother's smile was so wide I thought he'd break his face in half."

Bess laughed outright. "So might Vincent's in a week."

Amber turned her lips under. "I can't believe it. It's all happened so fast. I never thought I'd ever marry

89

before you. Look at you; you're practically a wife and mother already. So good with the kids and cooking and everything. I'm afraid I'm not gonna be much of a wife."

"Stop that, Amber Clarke. You'll be wonderful. You don't have to be like me. Vincent-Thomas Alexander doesn't love me; he loves Miss Amber Clarke, the feisty, spunky girl who isn't like anyone else. I love you, Amber, and I'm so thrilled for you."

"You sound almost wistful. I'm sorry things didn't happen for you and Nate. I feel guilty in some ways."

Bess frowned. "Why on earth would you feel guilty?" Maisy crawled up on her lap, and she put her arms around the girl and kissed her hair.

"Because here I am flaunting my happiness and...." She shrugged. "You don't even have a beau."

Another sting from Amber. Bess shook her head. "It's okay; I'm thrilled for you. I'm so glad you're happy. I can live vicariously through you."

"What about Nate?"

"What about him?" Bess frowned.

"Any likelihood of a reconciliation?"

"No, not unless something changes and he gives his heart to the Lord. I'm firm on that. I will not marry an unbeliever."

"But you love him, still?" Amber thrust her arms over her chest.

Bess nodded. "I'll always love him, I expect. If God wanted me to love someone else, He'd take these feelings from me. Perhaps He wants Nate to always be on my heart so I'll never stop praying for him, no matter what happens."

"So you wouldn't court anyone else?"

"Not as long as I'm in love with Nate. That wouldn't be fair on another man."

"What if he never converts and your feelings never leave?"

Bess shrugged and kissed the little girl again. "Then I suppose I'll never marry."

"But you'll be alone all your days, rather than be with the man you love, just because he's not a Christian."

"Yes, Amber. I stand by my conviction. God means more to me than anyone or anything else. And unless Nate shares that with me, I cannot and will not court him. If God wants me to fall in love with someone else, He will take this feeling from my heart and replace it with someone else."

"I don't understand. But I respect your conviction."

"Thank you. Anyway, this isn't about me; it's about you. One more week, and you'll be Mrs. Vincent Alexander."

Amber grinned. "Can you believe it? And we get to farm at your place! Oh, I wish you didn't have to leave the same day."

"I have to, Amber. I'm going with Aaron, Cass and the children to the city. Classes start in two weeks and Aaron needs the time to get acquainted. I'm going to help Cass with the kids until they settle and then go back to the estate with cousin Fred."

"How long before you move back here permanently?" Amber frowned.

Bess shrugged. "I'm really not sure. I may stay for the two years Aaron is there."

Amber's brows furrowed and she pouted. "Two years? You've already been gone nearly a year. I miss you so."

"You'll be far too busy living in wedded bliss to miss me, and it won't be forever. I'll be coming home, I promise."

"You'd better."

Maisy sat up. "Aun Bsss."

"Yes, my darling?"

"Dollsus."

"Dollhouse?"

The little girl nodded.

Bess grinned at her. "Okay, let's play with the dollhouse." She put Maisy down, and the little girl ran to sit on the mat in the corner.

"I'll go."

"You don't have to. You could play dollhouse with us?" Bess grinned.

"No thank you. I have a lot to do."

Bess bit her lip. "I bet you do. I can't wait for Saturday. You are going to be the most beautiful bride."

Both women stood up and embraced each other. "I love you, Bess. You're the best friend a girl could ever want."

"You too, Amber."

*   *   *   *

"Hello, Mr. & Mrs. Carter." Bess grinned widely as she greeted her brother and Cass on Saturday morning.

"Little Sister." Aaron was unable to stop smiling.

"You two look so happy." Bess embraced them both. "I'm so thrilled."

"We are. A little nervous about what the next few years hold, never thought I'd live in a city again." Cass chuckled.

"It's only for two years, Darling." Aaron squeezed her.

Bess gushed. "You two, you're so perfect together. Look at you; your faces are glowing,"

"Mama." Maisy came running out of the room.

She leaped into Cass's arms. "Ohhhh, my darling. I've missed you."

"Miss Mama." She kissed her Mama and then reached her arms out to Aaron. "Pa."

Aaron gulped and his eyes flooded with tears. It was the first time she'd called him that unsolicited. He reached for the girl and kissed her cheek. "Maisy, Darling, I missed you. I love you, Sweet Girl."

Maisy wrapped her arms around his neck. Bess and Cass both watched as Aaron swallowed back his tears again. He squeezed the little girl who he'd recently legally adopted.

Maisy sat back and kissed his cheek. "Love Dada."

"Oh, Darling, Dada loves you too." He grinned at the two women who had misty eyes. His eyes flicked from one to the other. "What?"

"It's just so beautiful to see a father loving his children. I'm just so delighted for you both. You have such a wonderful family, Aaron." Bess touched his arm.

He grinned. "How can I not love this little girl." He stroked Maisy's hair and kissed her cheek again. "I feel so overwhelmed and privileged to be her father, and that little boy."

Cass held Henry in her arms, and Aaron shifted Maisy to his hip to put his hand on Henry's back. "I can't wait to get on with being father and husband every day for the rest of my life." He grinned and winked at Cass.

"Me either, Husband. It's been a wonderful week, and I can't wait to see what the future holds. I can't believe tomorrow we'll be living in Chicago."

Aaron squinted at her. "No regrets?"

Cass lifted her free hand to his cheek. "I will follow you to the ends of the earth. I want you to do this. I want to see you live your dream. You need to be a doctor, Aaron. It's who you are."

Aaron closed his eyes. "I feel like I don't deserve this happiness." He stroked Maisy's hair again.

"Oh hush, you both deserve every bit of it." Bess grinned.

"So do you, Sister. I hope to see you just as happy someday." Aaron gave her a sad smile and squeezed her arm.

Bess shrugged. "I don't know what my future holds. But I am happy, Brother. Seeing you happy makes my heart sing. And if I marry one day, I hope I'll be just as happy as you. But if I don't, then that's the Lord's will, and I will go on serving Him till the day I die."

Aaron embraced his sister. "I love you, Bess."

"I love you, Aaron." She turned to embrace Cass. "I love you, too, Cass. I'm over the moon to have a sister at last."

"Me too. And I love you as well. Thank you for all you've done for us."

"No, you don't have to thank me. The fact that you make my brother grin like that, is all the thanks I ever need." She gestured to her brother.

Aaron just shrugged. He really couldn't argue. It was seldom these days that he didn't wear that smile. He couldn't even remember the darkness of old.

Bess stood back. "Pa would be proud of you, Joey and Ma, too."

"I hope so, Sister. Apart from God and you and this incredible woman, I live to make them proud."

Bess looked at the clock. "Oh, we'd better go. Amber will be getting married in an hour."

"And in six hours we'll be headed for Liberty to catch the train." Aaron grinned, showing the two women out. He closed the door behind him.

Ten

"You look like death warmed up." Nate scowled at Henry as he stumbled into work late for the fifth day in a row.

"Why didn't you wake me?"

Nate shrugged. "Why should I? You're a grown man. You can get yourself up, and off to work."

Henry groaned and slumped into his chair. "My head hurts."

"Well, if you laid off the whiskey, it wouldn't."

"You were drinking, too."

"Yeah, but I knew when to stop, can't afford to drink more than two anyway." He chuckled. "I'm coming up on having thirty dollars in my money tin."

"Henry!" A voice hollered from the office behind them.

Henry cringed. "Sounds like he's on the warpath today."

Nate shrugged. "I've heard him yell at three people. He was short with me too, and I was on time."

"What's got up his nose?"

"Henry, get your sorry backside in here!"

"Coming." Henry grimaced again and hurried into his father's office. "What is it?"

"Sit down." His father scowled at him.

Henry's smirk disappeared instantly and he thrust himself into the chair. His father was in one of those moods, and it was best not to mess with him.

Archibald Martin peered down his nose at Henry and fixed him in his steely glare. It didn't matter if this was his son. He was an employee and therefore worthy of his wrath. "Tell me about the Cameron account."

Henry's cheeks reddened. "What about it?"

"What is your understanding of what they wanted?"

"I... I'm not sure, Sir... Nate dealt with that account," Henry lied, terrified of what his father might do, if he found out Henry had come to work drunk every day that week.

"Nathaniel Sawyer?"

"Yes, Sir. He spoke to Mr. Cameron when he came in and typed the order and organized the shipment."

"Nathaniel sent three hundred rolls of silk to New York instead of thirty?"

Henry gulped. He must have been so addled from the alcohol that he'd misread the order. "Yes, that's correct, Sir. I bet if you ask him, he'll deny it. 'Cause he doesn't wanna get in trouble. He's scared of you, Sir."

"Get him in here."

Henry sped out of the office so fast he knocked over the chair. A pang of guilt struck him for putting this on Nate's shoulders. But he had too many black marks with his father already. Nate had proven himself diligent and honest and was one of the hardest workers in the company. He regularly outperformed Henry and the man had begun to build up a resentment towards his friend.

Father likes Nate, he'll just get a smack on the hand and docked wages. He'll bounce back.

97

"Nate. He wants to see you." Henry grimaced and sat back in his chair.

Nate stopped typing and looked up. "Me?" He frowned.

"Yeah, apparently you messed up an order."

Nate frowned. "I'm always very careful. I always double-check them." He stood.

"Sawyer, get in here," the voice bellowed.

Henry grimaced at his friend as he hurried past his desk. Another pang of guilt swept through him. He shrugged. *Perhaps if he wasn't so reliable and didn't show me up all the time with his country bumpkin 'honesty and hard work' philosophy, I wouldn't have put this on him.* He tried to justify his treachery.

"You wanted me, Sir?" Nate raised his brows as he entered the office.

Archibald scowled and nodded to the chair. Nate obliged, picking it up from the floor, setting it upright and taking the seat.

"You handled the Cameron account, is that correct?"

"I took the initial order, Sir, but I didn't send it off. Henry did that, as he no doubt told you."

Archibald squinted. He leaned forward on his elbows. "He said you'd deny it."

Nate frowned. "Deny what? I never sent their order, Sir. I'm very careful, and I always double-check. Henry sent that order, Mr. Martin, Sir. I swear it.

"I don't believe you, Sawyer. This your order?" The man held up the page – the order carefully typed in the right places.

Nate looked it over and nodded. "Yes, that's the order I typed, Sir."

"How many rolls of silk, does this order say?" He thrust his finger at the words.

"Thirty, Sir. I remember it well; the man told me they needed a big shipment of silk for his new bridal store in New York City."

Archibald squinted again. He was in a rage that day, intolerant of everyone and everything. Far too many orders were going astray, and it was costing him more than he could afford. Nobody knew just how close to bankruptcy the man was. His anger boiled over, and he'd been on the lookout for a scapegoat. This country boy would do just fine. He didn't care to investigate further. He was much too angry.

"Then why, Sawyer, did the man receive a shipment of three... hundred... rolls?" He scowled.

Nate's brows flew up, and he shook his head. "Three hundred, instead of thirty?"

"Don't be cute, Sawyer, and pretend you don't know. This was your order, you shipped it, and YOU are responsible for it." The man stood out of his chair and thrust his finger out at Nate. Hot, angry, and defeated, the man cursed twice and came around the desk. "You're gonna pay for this, Sawyer. That shipment cost me more money than you could count in a week." His cheeks reddened and the vein in his neck pulsed. He clenched his fists. Nate tried to speak, twice, but the man shut him down.

"I won't hear any pathetic attempts at justifying yourself, Sawyer. That's what I get for welcoming a poor country waif into my home and my business. I should have known you'd be the demise of this company." Archibald squinted and leaned forward as far as he could. He slapped the table loudly. "You're fired, Sawyer."

Nate gasped and his brows flew up. He knew that Henry had filed that order and assumed he'd told his father it was Nate to get himself out of hot water. "But, Sir, it was Henry...."

"Don't start with me, Sawyer. You can leave, without pay, and don't you dare step a foot in my house. I don't ever want to see you again. And, just so you know, I give hundreds of dollars to the University every year; there is a wing named after me. I'll see to it you don't get admitted to your second year of law school, and you'll never sit the bar in this state. An untrustworthy no-good like you will have no place in the law."

Nate's head dropped and he sucked in deep breaths. He desperately tried not to cry.

Henry heard every word through the wall, grimacing, he hung his head. He really hadn't expected that overreaction from his father. To fire Nate was one thing, and to kick him out another, but to stop him from finishing his law degree? The guilt began to overwhelm him.

Nate looked up at his boss and, squared his shoulders. "I'll go, Sir. I'm owed eight dollars."

The man stepped forward and squinted. "Oh, you're owed eight dollars, are you?" A look of pure hate crossed the older man's face. He jabbed a finger into Nate's chest. "You cost me nigh on two hundred dollars, and you are quibbling over eight. You'll get nothing from me. Get out of here before I have you whipped."

Nate swallowed, gave the man a nod, and fled. He made no eye contact with Henry. He thrust his coat off the hook and headed for the door.

"I'm sorry," Henry called.

Nate spun around and scowled at him. "You're sorry? You're sorry?" He shook his head. "Don't even start with me, Henry. I can't trust a man who'd treat a friend that way." Nate turned on his heels and marched out.

Stepping out into the August sunshine, he hung his head. He had no place to go, no job, and no money. He thrust his hands in his pockets and pulled out his two most precious treasures, his grandfather's pocketwatch and the bone-handled pocket knife he'd been given by his parents for his sixteenth birthday.

There was no way he was going back to the Martin estate to fetch his things, or his hard-earned savings in the tin beneath his bed. His law books were useless to him now. He hung his head and thrust his knuckles into the brick wall twice, tearing the skin almost to the bone. "Arrrrgghhh!" he cried out, a look of such anger on his face that a woman with a small boy, gasped and hurried to cross the street away from him. Nate sighed loudly and hung his head. "See, there is no God."

Taking off at a run, he made his way to the nearest saloon, slammed the watch and knife on the bar, and demanded, "As much whiskey as these will get me." He scowled at the barkeep.

Without looking up from the cup he was drying, the man responded, "We don't barter."

Nate squinted. "I said, as much whiskey as these will get me." He slammed his hand down on the bar.

"Alright, alright." The barkeep pulled the half-full bottle from the shelf and passed it and a glass to Nate.

Nate pushed the glass away and lifted the bottle to his lips.

Eleven

"I've really gotta go, Amber. I am sorry, but we have to catch the stage to Liberty to get the express in the morning."

"I don't ever want to let you go." Amber squeezed Bess tightly.

Bess pried herself from Amber's grip and stood back. She leaned in and kissed her friend on the forehead. "You are the most beautiful bride, and you're going to be so happy with your new husband." She gave her friend a sad smile and nodded to Vincent standing next to her. "I'm really gonna miss you." She touched both on the shoulder, swallowed her emotions, and hurried away to her waiting family, sighing loudly as she fell into step with them. Aaron shifted Maisy to his left hip and put his right arm around his sister's shoulder. "I'm sorry. I know leaving is hard."

"It isn't the leaving; it's what I have to leave behind. I love it here; I was just beginning to feel at home again."

"Well, why not stay? We can manage without you." Cass gripped her arm as they approached the stagecoach platform.

"Because I promised Cousin Frederick I'd come back. There is still much to do around the estate, and I want to get back to volunteering at the orphanage...."

"And Nate is there?" Aaron lifted a brow as he helped the women and children into the stage and leaped up behind them.

He took his seat next to Cass and looked at his sister. She hugged Maisy tightly on her lap and sighed. "I think that ship has sailed, I'm afraid. I don't even know where he is anymore. I called into his boarding house some time ago, and they told me he'd moved out." She shrugged. "No one knew where he'd gone. I guess he's moved on as well."

Aaron stretched across the coach to squeeze her hand. "I really am sorry. I get all this happiness, and you get nothing but sadness and hurt. It seems backwards somehow. I'm the one who deserved the sadness; I was so miserable all those years."

Bess flashed him a sad smile. "That's why you deserve all this happiness. And you don't have to be sorry. It's the way it is, and I'll be okay. I'm excited you will be in Chicago. It'll be an adjustment. Having people cook and clean and even help you with your clothing takes some getting used to."

Cass frowned. "What will I do all day?"

"You'll be a lady of leisure, Darling." Aaron grinned.

Cass screwed up her nose. "Sounds awfully boring. What do rich ladies do all day?" She tilted her head at Bess.

Bess cringed. "I'm not a rich lady. I don't know what they do either. They always seem to be at fundraisers or parties and cotillions, or spending hours in downtown stores. I was bored after two weeks. If it wasn't for Aunt Meredith, I'd've had nothing to do. I'm glad I have the work at the orphanage and for the church, and I lead three of Aunt Mere's charities too. It keeps me busy and I like to think I'm doing some good."

"You are. Those children are worth it." Cass grinned.

Bess smiled and leaned back against the seat. Maisy was asleep. They had a long trip to Liberty, an overnight stay, and a long train ride ahead of them. "Get comfortable. This is quite a trip." She grinned and laid her head back.

Cass nodded, checked on Henry in his basket on the floor, and leaned back into Aaron's arms. He grinned and kissed her hair. "Ahhh, just where I love you to be. Try to get some sleep, Darling."

She nodded and closed her eyes.

* * * *

Young seminary graduate Levi Simmons left the mission. He shook his head, pushed his unruly dark hair back off his forehead and sighed. *Lord, I pray we're doing some good. Those people are so broken and needy. Help us change their lives and bring them the gospel. I just want to serve You, Father. I want to be Your hands in this dark and broken city, as long as You need me here, or until You show me where You want me to be. I thank You for redeeming me from a life of sin and shame and for the many blessings You've given me.* A groan halted his prayer, and he paused, lifting his head to listen. There it was again; it sounded like it was coming from the alley behind the saloon.

He frowned and walked towards the sound. The lanternlight didn't reach that far and it was very dark. He could just make out the silhouettes of broken furniture and piles of trash. He screwed up his nose as he walked in, using his hands to help him avoid colliding with anything. *Breathe through your mouth,*

Levi. He heard the groan again. "Hello, is someone there?" He looked around, straining his eyes to see through the darkness. "Oh." He gasped, seeing the outline of a man. As his eyes began to adjust to the low light, he noticed the man was extremely battered, wearing nothing but his long underwear, torn in many places. His body lay at strange angles.

Levi knelt beside him. "Lord, help me." He placed a hand on the man's shoulder and he groaned. "I'm sorry." The shoulder was obviously dislocated. "Don't worry. I'll get you some help. The Lord will look after you until I return." He glanced to the heavens and hurried away.

*   *   *   *

"Oh, look at this place. I've never seen such a big house." Cass and Aaron both had wide eyes as they drove up the long cobbled driveway to the cottage.

Bess chuckled.

"What's so funny, Little Sister?"

"This is the small house. The estate is about five times the size."

Aaron's mouth fell. "I can't imagine that."

"Well, you'll see it soon enough. Come on, let's get you settled." She nodded to Knowles. "Please wait for me. I'll be an hour or so if you'd like to come and get a refreshment."

"Thank you, Ma'am; I'm happy waiting with the carriage. Send the hall boy to the stables when you are ready to go."

She nodded and smiled and the man clucked to the horses and drove away.

Aaron grinned at her.

"What?"

"You seem so at home with servants and decadence. I think you're a city girl at heart."

Bess grimaced. "No, I'm just accustomed to it. I still prefer the simple country life. Although I must say, I could get quite used to indoor plumbing."

Cass burst out laughing.

"Now come on. Jasper will be waiting."

Bess banged the knocker on the wide door. A starched-looking butler opened it. He smiled to Bess. "Mistress, welcome."

"Hello, Jasper."

"Please, won't you all come in." The butler pointed to the foyer. Eyes explored the wide walls; it was a miniature version of the estate, with brocade curtains and marble and gold fittings, paintings, and sculptures. Bess led them past the hall and into the parlor. Jasper closed the door and followed.

Bess turned to him. "Jasper, allow me to introduce my brother, and fellow owner of this house, Aaron Carter." She emphasized *owner* for both Jasper's and Aaron's sake. Aaron grimaced but didn't say a word. "This is his wife, Cass, and their children, Maisy and Henry."

Jasper tipped his head to them. "Sir, Madam, Jasper Coates at your service."

"Normally, staff are called by their last names, but Jasper is just... well, Jasper." Bess grinned.

"You need anything, day or night, pull that cord, and one of us will come." He gestured to the six people standing quietly by the wall.

Aaron and Cass turned their eyes to the people. Having 'staff' was going to take some adjusting too. Bess introduced them to the head housemaid, two maids, cook, hall boy, and footman, then dismissed them.

Aaron turned his eyes to her.

"I know what you're thinking. I didn't like the idea of having servants either, but I spoke to Crews; he's the butler at the estate. He said they want to work; it gives them satisfaction. The family has always treated them respectfully, and he felt pride that 'his' family was so well looked after. To them, it's no different to if they worked in a factory or at the mill. He said to let them go would be to deprive them of a job. They can be hard to get in this city. So please, let them do what they are paid to do. They get a very good salary, and they're hard workers. Cass, I know it's gonna take some getting used to, but it's only for a season."

Cass smiled and Aaron gave her a reluctant nod.

"Come on, I'll show you to your suite."

＊　　＊　　＊　　＊

"Bess, so good to have you back." Fred greeted her with an embrace.

She followed him into the sitting room, and he sent Crews to get them tea.

"So, are they all settled in the cottage?"

"Yes, it'll take them some getting used to."

"You adjusted; they will too."

"I have to admit, having servants doesn't really sit well with me."

"Don't think of them as servants; think of them as employees. They work for us, and they do a good job, and we pay them accordingly."

"Don't you tire of having people wait on you, hand and foot?"

"Not really, but then I don't know any different. I can see why it would be hard for you."

"I'm so used to doing everything myself. I was reminded of that when I went home. In some ways, I really miss it. Even though it's hard work, it's satisfying knowing you take care of what's yours. This lifestyle is particularly hard for women. We don't go off to the factory every day. It's hard to find things to do. Cass will find it hard to begin with."

"She's got the little ones to take up her time."

"Of course. And I'm sure I'll see them most days. Maisy and Henry are dear children. I miss them already."

"Do you regret coming back here?"

"No, they deserve to have the house to themselves. Besides, you need me, so here I'll be."

"I'm glad, Bess. I know I can't keep you forever, and I came to terms with that while you were gone. But however long you are here, I will be grateful."

"We need to work on finding you a wife, Cousin, so you won't be so lonesome."

He grimaced. "I'm open to suggestions."

Bess chuckled.

*   *   *   *

"He's waking up." Levi poked his head out to the waiting room to summon his father and brother.

The three men hurried back to the stranger's bedside. Levi had not left his side in two days, except for a few moments to eat and refresh. He'd stayed and prayed constantly for the stranger. The man was in a bad way, with several broken bones, dislocated shoulder, bruises, cuts and scratches. He'd needed several rows of stitches and had been unconscious since Levi had brought him in.

The doctor stood over the man. He groaned and turned his head. His sore arm moved and he groaned again. At last, his eyelids fluttered open and he looked around, his disoriented brain trying to comprehend what was happening.

"Can you hear me?" the doctor asked.

"Yes." The man's head pounded and he squinted against the light.

"I'm Doctor Allen Little. You're in the hospital. It looks like you took quite a beating."

The man turned his head to look around. There was a pastor and two other men in the room. He squinted at them, trying to make sense of it all in his hazy mind.

Levi smiled kindly. "We found you behind the saloon on Broadstreet. We brought you here two nights ago."

The man shook his head slightly.

"What's your name?" The doctor held his hand to the man's neck, held up his pocketwatch, and tested the pulse rate.

"Na..." The man's lips struggled to form the words. He blinked and ran his dry tongue over them. "Nathan... Nate," he managed.

The doctor nodded. "Well, Nate, you've got some nasty injuries, but I'm confident you'll recover in time."

"Th..." He exhaled. "Thank you, Doctor."

"Sore head?"

Nate nodded slightly.

"I'll send a nurse in with something to help you sleep." The doctor looked up at Levi. "Why don't you all go on home? He's got a bit of recovering to do."

"I want to stay."

The doctor nodded to Levi. "Please yourself."

Nate grimaced. His muddled brain was unable to understand why these strangers wanted to help him. "I'm sorry," he whispered.

"Why are you sorry?" Levi asked, lifting his own glass of water to Nate's parched lips and lifting his head to help him drink.

"You've... you've had to... help me."

"Nate. It's our pleasure. I'm glad we've got a name to call you now." Levi smiled kindly. "You focus on getting well; then we'll find a way to get you home."

Nate closed his eyes. He groaned. "No... I have no home. No... money... clothes."

Levi smiled kindly and touched his shoulder. "Don't you worry. We'll make sure you're taken care of."

"That's right, Son, you just concentrate on getting well." Mr. Benjamin Simmons nodded at his two sons.

"I have no... way to pay..." Nate's ribs were on fire, his broken leg agonising, and every breath was painful. As his foggy brain became more lucid, he registered more of the pain.

"It's okay, Nate. The Lord provides. He will make a way," Mr. Simmons assured him.

Nate grimaced and closed his eyes. *He's never made a way for me before.* His brain protested. Still, he had no choice but to trust these people.

"Sleep, now. I'll be right here." Levi nodded.

His father and brother turned to leave. "We best get back; Ma will be worried."

"Okay, tell her I'm staying here as long as I'm needed." Levi sat back in his chair.

"I will, Son. The Lord is with you. We'll be prayin'."

"Thanks, Pa." The young pastor nodded and the men left.

"You... don't need to... stay."

Levi leaned forward and put his hand on Nate's good shoulder. "I'm not leaving you alone. Everyone needs someone to rely on. I'll be here as long as you need me."

Nate gave him the slightest nod. A nurse arrived and gave him some pain relief. "Sleep now. I'll be by to check on you later."

"Sawyer... Nate Sawyer," he managed.

"I'm Nurse Wright. You sleep, Mr. Sawyer." She smiled kindly, picked up the empty glass, and left.

Nate felt awfully sleepy as he listened to Levi's quiet voice while he read from the Scriptures. "The Lord is my Shepherd; I shall not want. He maketh me to lie down in green pastures: He leadeth me beside the still waters. He restoreth my soul: He leadeth me in the paths of righteousness for His name's sake. Yea, though I walk through the valley of the shadow of death, I will fear no evil; for Thou art with me; Thy rod and Thy staff they comfort me....."

For Thou art with me? Are you God? Nate fell asleep with that thought running through his mind.

*   *   *   *

"So, how are you settling in?" Fred nodded his thanks to Jasper, who delivered their drinks, and turned back to his cousins.

"Fine, thank you, you've been most kind." Cass smiled.

"It's not me, Ma'am. This home belongs to you and Bess. It's me that should be grateful to you, for welcoming me in."

"It's our pleasure, Cousin Fred." Aaron kissed the head of the little girl, sound asleep in his arms.

Fred grinned. "That's a little different from your last greeting."

Aaron grimaced. "I'm sorry about that. It's fair to say, I'm a little different since my last greeting to you."

"Yes, Bess has kept me abreast of all that's been happening. I was delighted to hear of your marriage and your heartfelt commitment to the Lord. I too recently joined the fold."

"Glad to hear it, Cousin." Aaron grinned. "And thank you. We are very happy."

"I'm a little envious." Fred looked across at Bess, with Henry in her arms. "I've been telling Bess I hope to find a lovely lady myself. But unlike most in my circles, I refuse to marry if not for love. Sadly despite the size of this city, there seems to be slim pickings." He laughed, but he looked a little wistful.

"We'll pray you find the right woman, Fred." Cass looked at her husband and squeezed his hand. "Nothing sweeter than a good marriage."

Aaron winked and carefully leaned over without disturbing Maisy to kiss his wife on the cheek. "Nothing sweeter indeed."

Fred nodded. "So, how are you finding college?"

Aaron's face lit up. "It's only been two weeks, but I've already learned so much. I'm really enjoying it, except for the time I spend away from my family."

Cass squeezed his arm supportively. "We're happy to make the sacrifice, Husband. We want this as much as you do." She turned to Fred. "He comes home full of life, and tells us all about his learning. Just as well for him; I'm not the squeamish type."

Everyone chuckled.

"I'm glad you got the scholarship. It means you don't have to work, that means more time with your family." Fred grinned and drained his tea cup. He placed it on the table next to him.

Maisy woke up and sat back from Aaron, rubbing her eyes. "Did you have a good sleep, my darling?" He stroked her hair back off her face.

Maisy nodded. "Dweem Charwee."

"You dreamed about Charlie dog?"

"Mmmhmmm."

"I know you miss him, Darling, but Aunty Amber is taking excellent care of him back on the farm."

"Sad, Charwee."

"I'm sure he misses you too."

Maisy rubbed her eyes again and looked around. "Huwoo." She nodded at Fred.

"Hello, Miss Maisy. Good to see you again." He really didn't know how to address children.

Maisy climbed down off Aaron's knee and hurried over to the dollhouse they had carefully packaged and brought with them. She picked up the peg people and chatted while she played.

Aaron watched her and shook his head. The look in his eye made Bess grin and sniff away a tear. It was so precious to see her beloved brother adoring his wife and children. A deep longing grew in her for a family of her own. *I really do want that. Your will be done, Lord.* She sighed.

Aaron turned back to Fred. "I want to thank you for your part in getting my scholarship. I'm much obliged to you."

"Of course. My pleasure. I'm just glad I could help. My father donated a lot of money to the university, so the name Bennett gave me some clout."

"Thank you for using your clout for me."

Fred nodded. He, too, looked at the family nostalgically, wishing for a family of his own.

115

Twelve

"Here is the bill for two weeks hospital care, Mr. Simmons."

Benjamin took the slip of paper and grimaced. He passed it to Levi and he frowned. "We can cover it, Pa. The Lord will provide."

He nodded. "We'll find that money, but we might not be able to from here on." Benjamin frowned. "What are we going to do?"

Levi looked up at the doctor. "Is he able to go home? We could continue his care."

The doctor screwed up his nose. "Not really, he ought to stay here, but I understand your predicament, and I'm sure you can manage Mr. Sawyer's care at home, amongst you. You've been here most days and seen what I've been doing."

"We'll take him home today." Levi looked to his father for approval.

Ben nodded and smiled kindly. "Of course, Son. I'll bring the wagon, and tell Ma to prepare a space for him."

"Nate can have my bed, I'll share with Amos," Levi offered without hesitation. "Pa, will you bring some of my clothing for him? We can't take him home in his long underwear."

"Of course, Son." Ben turned to the doctor. "I'll be back in a few hours, and I'll bring you the money then."

"Very well. I'll see you then, Mr. Simmons."

Ben smiled and left the room.

The doctor turned to Levi. "Come on back to Mr. Sawyer's room, and I'll talk you through his long-term care."

Levi smiled and stood. He followed the doctor out.

*   *   *   *

"What, where am I?" Nate looked around. He was in a house in a bedroom, rather than the hospital. He turned his head to see Levi seated by his bed.

"You're at our home, Nate. We had to bring you home, but you can stay just as long as you need to."

Nate smiled. "I don't know how to thank you."

"You can thank us by getting well." Levi placed his hand on Nate's shoulder and smiled kindly.

Nate closed his eyes. *Why are they so kind?* He sighed. *They remind me so much of Bess.*

Mr. Simmons entered with a glass of water. "Oh, good you're awake. How are you feeling?"

"Sore. But better than last week."

"You up to telling us what happened?" Levi and Ben helped Nate sit up. He winced in pain as his strapped broken leg dragged up the bed and his ribs ached. But sitting up was a relief. He gritted his teeth and was at last propped up on some pillows. Ben passed him the glass of water.

Nate took a long drink. "Well..." He began with a loud sigh. He unfolded the entire story, all that had happened with Bess, his friend's betrayal, being fired, and his choice to get drunk.

Levi nodded and stroked his chin. "You've had a time of it for sure. I'm sorry about your girl. I do happen to think she's right in her convictions. If she loves you as you say she does, then she'll be hurting as much as you do."

Nate shrugged one shoulder. "I'm sure she's moved on and married by now. She's much too sweet for men not to notice her." He sighed.

Levi smiled and gripped Nate's shoulder. "I really am sorry. She sounds like a lovely girl."

Nate gave him a sad smile. "The loveliest. I can't be angry at her." He shrugged. "I admire her conviction...."

"But you're still in love with her?"

Nate nodded. "Yeah, can't seem to get her out of my mind or heart."

"I'll pray for you. And her. You never know what the Lord might do."

Nate screwed up his face. "Don't bother; God's turned His back on me."

Levi gave him a compassionate smile. "There is not a wretch in this world that the Lord has given up on. Trust me, Nate; He redeemed me."

"You? But you're a pastor?"

Levi nodded. "I wasn't always."

Nate raised his brows.

"In a nutshell, I rebelled, alcohol, loose women, gambling, all of it." He shook his head sadly, full of regret over his past indiscretions.

Nate frowned. "But you don't look any older than me."

"I'm twenty-two. I ran away when I was not yet sixteen, felt too much pressure to be a good Christian boy, I guess. The Lord found me, much the same as I found you, in a gutter, with nothing to show for it except bad memories and brokenness. I came home to plead forgiveness, and my parents welcomed back their prodigal with open arms. I turned back to the Lord and vowed that day that I would dedicate my life to serving Him. He called me to be a pastor and I'll do all I can to help my fellow wretches."

"I sure am one of those." Nate sighed loudly.

"You didn't tell me how you got from the saloon to the alley."

Nate grimaced. "It's hazy. I can't remember all of it. I know I was gambling. I had nothing to play with, but they let me build up a substantial debt. I was well on my way to drunk, and they kept the whiskey coming deliberately. When I lost, and I couldn't pay, they told me they'd take it out on my hide. I think that was their plan all along; they seemed to be itching for a fight all evening. They beat me black and blue, stripped me of all my clothing, and left me for dead. They took the photo of Bess from my pocket. I've always carried it, although I'm not sure why. I just have to close my eyes, and I can see her." He sighed.

"Do you know who they were?"

Nate shrugged. "Could've been anyone. I was well inebriated at that time."

Levi nodded. "I'm sorry. I'm sorry you lost everything too."

"I'm not sure what I'm going to do now, or how I'm going to pay you back." Nate sighed.

"Don't worry about that. You can stay here as long as you need to. Doc says you can get up soon, hopefully, now that your leg is healing and you're feeling a little better."

Nate nodded at Mr. Simmons. "I'm most grateful to you. As soon as I'm out of this bed, I'll do what I can to pull my weight. I don't want charity. A man needs to earn his own way."

Ben Simmons nodded. "I understand, Nate, but everyone needs charity at times. There is no shame in letting others help you."

Nate chuckled. "Bess said that to me once."

"She's right. Everyone needs help. The way you repay that is to help others. Serving others can be rewarding," Levi added.

"She said that, too." Nate gave a wry smile and yawned.

"We'll leave you to sleep." Ben nodded to his son.

Levi stood. "I'll be by to check on you in a few hours."

Nate nodded. The two men helped him to lie back in the bed and left the room. He laid back on the pillow, his ribs ached, his leg was on fire and he was far from healed. He looked around. The room was small and rather crude; it appeared to have once been a large cupboard or small storage room. Long marks ran across the wall running parallel with nail holes where the shelves had been removed to fit the bed in. He would never guess he was in Chicago if he didn't know better. It looked a lot like some of the houses back home. There was little decoration, a small bed with a wobbly table next to it, one leg propped up on a piece of folded paper. It was just big enough for a basin and jug. A wardrobe was squeezed in at the foot of the bed, and there was a trunk in the corner that one had to shimmy around carefully to enter the room; it doubled as a chair. A Bible sat in the middle of it.

It was obvious the family was very poor. He lifted the thin sheets and homemade crazy quilt and noticed the clothing someone had dressed him in, it was somewhat tatty but clean and dry. The trousers had patches sewn into the knees, and the shirt had two mismatched buttons.

He sighed. *These people don't have much, yet they've rescued me, fed me and clothed me, paid my medical bills, and even bathed me. Why would they do that when I can't possibly ever repay them?*

He shrugged and smiled. *Bess is like that too. Always giving to others, and she didn't have much either. What do they have in common?* His eyes fell on the Bible. *God.* He grimaced. Why was it that people who followed God, devout followers, were so generous and giving? Bess had told him that those who had been forgiven much should forgive much. She often said, "there but for the grace of God, go I." She'd suffered so much but was kind and generous.

Nate sighed. "God," he said aloud. "I want to believe. If you really are who you say you are, show me." He closed his eyes and drifted off to sleep.

* * * *

121

"This is going to be the best Christmas yet." Bess placed a large sprig of pine on the mantle at the cottage.

"Yes, it'll be wonderful. I'm glad to share it with family." Cass placed the last of the candles on the side table. Staff were busy climbing ladders and putting up ribbons and pine branches. A large tree almost reached the ceiling, trimmed with ornaments and ribbons.

"I'm looking forward to it. I was so lonesome for Aaron last year. I never dreamed this year he'd have a family in tow." Bess laughed as Maisy twirled a ribbon over her head. "I do so love the chatter and laughter of children." She sighed.

"You'll have your own someday, Bess." Cass walked over and touched her hand. "You're still young."

"Thank you, Cass. You're a good friend. I'm so glad to have you as a sister."

Cass wrapped her in a warm embrace. "You too, Bess. I couldn't be more blessed than to be a part of this family."

Bess looked at her. "I am sorry that you lost Henry though. I don't wish that on anyone."

Cass nodded and gave her a sad smile. "Thank you. Henry is a pleasant memory from my past. I loved him, and I'll always love him in a way, but as a memory to keep alive for Maisy and Henry. But I never loved him the way I love Aaron. Our love is so fierce and strong it knocks me off my feet sometimes."

Bess sighed. She closed her eyes and her lips trembled. "That's how I feel about Nate; like my whole body is on fire. The more I try not to love him the more

I love him. I don't understand why God won't take these feelings from me." A tear streaked down her cheek.

"Maybe he wants you to love him in the future. He's just waiting for Nate to be ready." Cass squeezed her arm.

"Maybe, but I don't think Nate's ever going to accept God." She shrugged and wiped at her eyes. "I'm sorry, Cass. It's sinful of me to despair over a forbidden love."

"Bess, you are only human." Cass covered her mouth and clutched the edge of the table.

"That's for sure. Oh, what's the matter?"

Cass stood up and gave her a sheepish grin, biting her lips together tightly and blushing a deep red.

Bess tilted her head and squinted.

Cass couldn't resist a wide grin.

Bess's face lit up. "No!"

Cass nodded and put her hand on her abdomen.

"No!" Bess shook her head. "Already?"

"It was a surprise to me too, but we have been married five months."

"Yeah, I guess you have. Oh, I'm so thrilled for you."

"Our children will be very close together."

"Does Aaron know?"

"No, and please don't spoil it. I plan to tell him Christmas morning."

"What a Christmas blessing. Oh, Cass." Bess's eyes filled with tears. "I am so happy for you both. Aaron is going to be over the moon."

Cass grinned. "Yes, he's already a wonderful father. He's delighted with the family we have. But I know he'll love whoever comes along."

Bess squeezed her arm and jumped and clapped. She stopped abruptly as Aaron walked in with a sleepy boy in his arms. He squinted at them. "What's going on in here, you two?"

Bess just shrugged and reached for the baby. She paced away, cooing to the little boy.

"Cass?" Aaron folded his arms over his chest and pursed his lips comically at her.

"Mmmm." She already knew the secret wasn't going to last till the morning. She was bursting to tell him.

"What are you hiding, Mrs. Carter?"

"It's a secret." She tucked her lips under, lest she just blurt it out.

He frowned. "There are no secrets between married people. Come on, out with it. Whatever it is, you can tell me, Darling." He reached for her hand and lifted the other to her cheek. "You are so beautiful, your skin is glowing, and your eyes are shining."

She grinned at him, and her face lit up all the more. "And I'm queasy to the stomach, experiencing vomiting, often in the mornings. I've been extra tired and emotional lately...." She bit her lip and stepped back.

Aaron furrowed his brow.

Cass tipped her head to the side and gave him a coy smile. "What's your diagnosis, Doctor?"

Aaron frowned again and looked from her to his sister's beaming face. He dropped his jaw to his chest. "Cass, are you..." he gulped, and tears raced to the corners of his eyes.

Cass nodded. "Yes, Pa. I'm two months along, I went to the doctor this morning, and he confirmed it."

Aaron yelled, "Yeeehaa," and jumped up as high as he could, punching the air. He lunged for Cass and pulled her close. "Oh, my darling. Ohhhh, this is the best news."

Cass looked up at him, her caramel eyes shining in joy. "I was going to wait to tell you on Christmas morning, but I saw your face, and I couldn't resist. I'm so excited."

Aaron sniffed away the tears. "Me too, Darling. I'm beyond excited; I'm thrilled. I was delighted with the two children we have, but now there will be more love and more joy to go around."

"You aren't worried that our children will be so close together? Three children under four?" She grimaced.

Aaron squinted at her. "Worried? Not at all, my darling. I'll love whoever comes along, whenever they come. I just love you so very much." He pulled her close and kissed her deeply. Then standing back, he placed his hand on her abdomen. "And I love you so much, Baby Carter."

Bess lay the baby in his crib and walked over. She looked at her brother with a wide smile and shining eyes. Neither said anything. "Oh, Aaron," was all she could manage.

He lunged for her too, lifted her off her feet, and spun her around. "Bess, I can't believe it."

"Congratulations to you both." She put an arm around each and kissed first her brother on the cheek and then Cass. "I love you both so much, and I can't wait to meet my newest niece."

"Niece, it's a girl?" Aaron furrowed his brow.

Cass chuckled. "You know it's impossible to tell. That's just Bess's wishful thinking."

"I don't mind if it's a girl." Aaron chuckled.

Cass raised a hand to his face. "I want to give you a son. A brave, strong boy who will grow up to be just like his pa."

Aaron kissed her again. "I'll love them whoever they are."

The three stood in a huddle for a time until a cry from the crib interrupted them.

"Merry Christmas." Bess grinned and headed for the cradle.

"Merry Christmas." Aaron kissed his wife again.

Thirteen

"Careful, one step at a time." Levi and Ben put their arms around Nate's shoulders, and waist and helped him hobble on his still weak leg, down the very narrow and rickety stairs to the sparsely decorated living room.

Looking around, Nate couldn't help but notice that his observations had been correct. This family didn't have much. The living room and dining room were one room. There were two mismatched couches, one with the stuffing sticking out and the other worn and stained. The carpet rugs were threadbare. A brick fireplace was the only source of heat and had a large pot hanging over it, with the stew cooking inside. The kitchen was primitive, with a few small cupboards and a makeshift wooden countertop. The pump was in the back yard so the water had to be brought in by the pailful. One end of the living room had a doorway with a curtain hanging across the opening, into the room where Ben and Angie slept and where the family kept their stores of canned food and the few spare blankets.

This house is so bare, but so full of joy and love. Levi helped Nate to the couch and leaned his crutch against the wall. The other four boys sat around on the floor or couches. Angie walked over, with a starched apron over her dress. "I'm so glad you made it down to join us, Nathaniel. Everyone should be with family for Christmas."

He gulped. "I'm grateful to you all."

127

"Think nothing of it. It's our pleasure to have you share the wonderous joy of Christmas with us." The woman smiled, pulled up an overturned nail box within his reach, and placed his coffee cup on it.

Nate nodded his thanks and grimaced as he leaned forward to pick it up. They had a very small Christmas tree, that was little more than a shrub, decorated with handmade paper chains and ornaments. Six stockings hung from the mantel, each newly knitted in a different color. The room was cozy, and all eyes shone with joy as the family gathered around.

Ben Simmons reached for the leather-bound book from the high shelf above the dining table and sat down on the couch between Nate and Levi. He opened the blessed book and read the account of Christ's birth from the Gospel of Luke.

All faces beamed as they listened to the blessed words. As well as Levi there was Amos, who was nineteen, sixteen-year-old Seth, thirteen-year-old Jonathan, and Little Davey, who was just ten. Lips recited together, "Behold, I bring you good tidings of great joy."

Nate had heard the story many times but never had he seen people's eyes shine like that, except for Bess. He could see her eyes clearly in his mind's eye, blue and shimmering with grateful tears as she spoke about the blessed Christ child. He sighed. There she was again, invading his thoughts. He inadvertently sniffed away a tear with the realization that he was more touched by the story than he'd ever been. Finally, Ben closed his Bible, and Levi led the family in a heartfelt prayer.

Mrs. Simmons began to sing. "Angels we have heard on high..." in a sweet and melodious voice. The family picked up the song with her. Nate stumbled along, singing the words he remembered.

Bess floated into his mind again; he could see her singing at the town Christmas celebration, her face alight with joy. It was her favorite song, and he could hear her sweet voice clearly in his mind as the family sang together. They went on to sing 'Joy to the World' and 'Silent Night' as well.

Another tear escaped Nate's eye. He swiped it away before anyone noticed. Sipping at his coffee, he looked around the room. They'd given him the best clothing from what they had, the only mug without a chip in it. He was sitting in the warmest place in the room, on the one couch cushion that wasn't stained or threadbare. He had a full cup of coffee; the rest of the cups were only half full. *They've given me the best of what they have.* He shook his head and sucked in the emotions.

"And now for gifts." Mrs. Simmons looked at the two smaller boys seated on the floor.

"May I, Ma?" David leaped up, with shining eyes.

"Of course, Davey."

"Mr. Sawyer, first." He smiled.

Nate frowned. "Oh, that's not necessary." His eyes grew misty as Davey reached for the navy blue stocking and passed it to him.

"Wait, and we'll all open them together." The boy smiled.

Nate merely nodded, swallowing rapidly, desperately burying down the emotions that bubbled up.

Soon all five boys and Nate had stockings on their laps.

"Okay, open them." Mrs. Simmons eyes glowed.

Nate waited and watched as each of the five boys pulled out a new knitted hat, scarf, and mittens in the same color as their sock. Nate looked in his stocking and found the same in a deep navy blue. He pulled them out and looked around. "What, this is..." he meant to protest, but seven joyous faces watched him, and he could see the delight it brought to them to give him these simple gifts. He smiled and sniffed. "These are wonderful, thank you." He immediately put the hat on his head, threw the scarf around his neck, and slipped his hands into the mittens. "Perfect fit, and so warm." He fought the tears, but his voice trembled. "Thank you for your kindness."

"Wait, there's more." Davey reached into his stocking and pulled out a small bundle wrapped in fabric. He opened it to find a decorated Christmas cookie. Davey's face lit up and he licked his lips. "Thank you, Ma." The other five stockings revealed their sugary treats too.

Mrs. Simmons beamed in joy. "Oh, you're welcome, Son. There is one very special extra thing this year. Have a look. It's different for each of you."

The boys all looked at each other; this was new.

"Davey, you start."

Davey reached to the bottom of the sock and pulled out the other green sock of the pair, as was the tradition. A new pair of socks each year, used as their Christmas stockings. Under the sock, he noticed something shine. He put his hand in and pulled out a tin whistle. "Wow." He held it up and played a jaunty little tune. "Thanks, Ma. Thanks, Pa." He embraced each.

"You are welcome, my music-loving son." Ben nodded to him and kissed his hair.

Davey sat back down and turned to Jonathan. "Your turn, Jon." He grinned.

Jonathan nodded and reached in to pull out his other sock, in a deep burgundy, and a new writing pen and ink pot. His eyes lit up. "Thank you, now I won't have to worry about the pencil not being sharp." Jonathon loved to write.

Seth's gift was a real leather belt, the first he'd ever owned. His father had made it from left over leather from his shoe store. Seth grinned and stood, pulled the piece of twine out of his trousers, and replaced it with the leather belt. His eyes shone. Amos got a slingshot. Davey laughed when he pulled it out. "It should be mine; I'm David."

They all chuckled, and their eyes swung to Levi. He smiled and put his hand in his sock. Under his second brown sock was a small leather-bound notebook with his name etched on the front. "It's for your prayers, Son."

"Thanks, Ma. I do like to write them down at times."

"You can use my ink pen," Jonathon offered. Levi reached over and scruffed his hair. Jonathan scowled at him.

Nate sat wide-eyed. The reaction to such small and relatively inexpensive gifts mystified him. The previous Christmas, he'd witnessed Henry's spiteful ungratefulness at the costly gifts he was given, but the joy these people had, despite having so little, really touched him. He gulped back a sob.

"Now you, Nate." Amos gestured to the sock on his knee.

"Oh." He was shocked that there was more for him too. He pulled out the second blue sock, and slid his hand back in and pulled out a little book. It was the Gospel of Luke. He lifted it out, and tears sprung to his eyes. He blinked them back. "I don't know what to say." He was much too overwhelmed.

Ben looked at him and put a hand on his shoulder. "Don't say anything, Son. Just read that little book. It'll do ya heart good."

Nate exhaled loudly and nodded. "I will. Thank you."

"It's our pleasure, Nathaniel. It's a joy to share Christmas with you." Ben squeezed the shoulder he still held and smiled kindly.

The boys immediately began to eat the brightly decorated Christmas cookies, a real treat, sugar was used sparingly in their home and saved for making bread, but each Christmas, Mrs. Simmons splashed out to make special cookies for the family and decorated them. Ben and Angie sat back with beaming smiles and hearts full of joy. Suddenly Nate felt a wave of overwhelming feelings surge through him, he sucked in two loud breaths and tears flooded his eyes.

Levi patted his back and fetched his handkerchief. The stitching was coming off, but it was clean. He passed it to Nate and the young man wiped at his eyes. Ben raised his brows. "What touches you, Son?"

"I don't know, really. What is it about you all? You have practically nothing, and yet you've given me so much, the best of all you have. You are so happy with your few gifts, and yet so many I've met are less than thankful in their abundance."

Ben put his arm around Nate. "We don't have much, Nathaniel, but the Lord has blessed us indeed. We have a lot more than many - a roof over our heads, food in our bellies, love, laughter, our family all together, the Word of God, and the blessing of your company. What more could we need?"

"But you can't afford this." He lifted the gifts up. "My hospital care, all you've given me. I don't understand. When you need it so badly yourself, why would you take me in and give me gifts, the same as your own sons?" His tears flowed uninhibited down his cheeks. "I've never known people like you." He grinned. "Except for Bess."

"It's the Lord, Nate." Levi nodded toward his father's Bible. "Won't you let Him in? He makes all the difference, and He wants to heal your soul, to walk with you all your days, and show you the way to love and serve others. Because in loving others, we love Christ."

Ben took over. "He tells us to love one another. So what you see here, Son, ain't nothing but Christian love.

God lavishes His grace and mercy on us, and so we give it to you, within the means God gives us to do so."

Nate buried his head in his hands and broke down in sobs. His wretched soul crying out for such a grace as these humble people had shown him. He sighed and shook his head. "I'm such a wretched and sinful man. I don't know why God would give me grace, but I'd sure like to know." He looked up at Levi and smiled through his tears. "Would you show me how?"

Levi grinned and slapped Nate on the back "I'd be delighted." Together the family, right down to young Davey, took Nathaniel into the scriptures. He'd heard so many of them before during his childhood, but now he saw them in a different light. He felt, for the first time, the words sink deep into his soul. At last, they bowed their heads and Levi led Nate in a prayer. He continued to sob as he prayed the words of repentance and hope. Then the family stood around him, put their hands on him, and each prayed for the lost sheep, brought back into the fold.

Nate opened his eyes after the final Amen. Every eye was full of tears, and they each embraced him. "Welcome to the family of God, Son. This is the best Christmas gift we could have asked for. I'd happily go without for the rest of my days for this one gift." Ben brushed away his tears. "To see any lost soul come to salvation is our greatest joy." He gripped Nate's shoulder firmly.

Nate's eyes shone and his soul soared. He breathed deeply, and despite his bruised ribs, he felt free and light for the first time in his life. He could see what Bess had been trying to tell him all along.

I'm sorry I didn't listen to you, Bess, you were right, and I was too stubborn to see it. Now I've lost you forever. Lord, I pray wherever Bess is tonight that you bless her. If she is married, bless her husband and family. Thank You for allowing me to know such an amazing woman. It is her influence that has led me here.

Fourteen

"You're quiet, Lad?" Ben Simmons turned to look at Nate as they sat to lunch a few weeks into February.

"I was just thinking about the message at church today. You know I went to church my whole life, and it never spoke to my soul the way your message did this morning, Levi. You're a gifted teacher."

Levi smiled. "I thank you, but the gift is from the Lord. I was terribly shy as a boy and even had a stutter. God has given me the ability to communicate His word."

"Well, it touched me to my soul. It's a new feeling for me. I've been a believer a few months now and I've never felt so free."

Angie reached across to touch his arm. "We can see that in your eyes, Son, and we're right pleased."

Nate dipped his bread in the soup and shoved it in his mouth. "Mmm. This is delicious, Mrs. Simmons. I thank you."

"You're welcome, Nate. We do the best we can with what we have."

Nate sighed. "I've been thinking it's time I move on."

All eyes spun to him. Ben put his spoon in his bowl, sloshing some soup over the side onto the table. He grimaced at his wife; she wordlessly stood, fetched a cloth, and wiped it up. Ben winked at her and turned to Nate. "Why?"

"I'm finally healed now, able to care for myself. You can't afford to keep me forever." He sighed. "I was thinking I might go home. I can't go back to college, least not in Chicago. So I guess I'll go back and work on my Pa's farm. Only... I don't have the means to get home."

Ben fixed kind eyes on Nate. "Nathaniel, you can stay here just as long as you need. We can afford to look after you, because the Lord will provide. We understand if you wanna go home, but don't do it because you feel like you are a burden to us. You aren't. You are as much family as our own boys."

Nate smiled. He scooped another soup-dipped piece of bread into his mouth. He nodded to Ben and looked around the very cramped table. His voice trembled. "I'm most grateful to you all; you've become like family to me too. I've been so touched by your love, and I'll always be grateful to you for introducing me to a loving Savior." He wiped away a tear. "You are amazing examples of servants of Jesus. I'll never forget you."

Ben gripped his shoulder and nodded.

"Still." Nate scratched his chin. "I really ought to start contributing and paying my way. I think I ought to find another job. I've been grateful to help in your store but I should find a paying job and give some money back to you, and earn my train fare home."

Ben and Angie looked at each other, communicating without words as they so often did. Angie looked at Nate. "We won't accept none of your money, Nate. If you want to contribute, give the money to the church for the needy. But if you want train fare home, we'll do what we can to help you with that when the time comes. We hope you won't hurry. We like having you here.

Watching you grow in your faith every day is a real delight to us."

Nate swallowed. "I've been so grateful to Levi for taking me into the Scriptures each day. It's coming alive to me in ways I never imagined possible."

"The Word of God is like that." Levi smiled. "Gets ahold of ya and doesn't ever let go."

"You ought to have a congregation of your own, Levi. You'd be a wonderful church pastor. There are so many wretches like me that need the word of God." Nate nodded to his friend.

Levi nodded. "I've actually been thinking on that myself. I think I'd like to find a little town like yours and serve God however I can."

Nate cleaned his bowl with his last piece of bread and held it in mid-air on the way to his mouth. "Wherever you go, the congregation will be blessed by your words. I sure will miss you, though." He slipped the bread in his mouth.

"Well, no decisions need to be made yet. It'll be months before we can arrange anything anyway. I'll check the ads at the seminary. They're usually up to date on who's looking for a pastor."

"I'll pray for you." Nate grinned.

"So will we, Son." Ben smiled. "We'll miss ya, but you have to be about the Lord's business. No matter where ya go, He's with ya. Whether it be a shoe store like mine, a ma in the house, boys at school, or a pastor or lawyer, we are all about the Lord's business."

Nate nodded. *I want to be able to use my abilities for You, Lord. Guide me to know the plans You have for me.*

* * * *

Nate stood and wiped his brow. He placed the axe against the wall and looked toward his boss. "I appreciate you giving me this job, Sir."

Mr. George Long swished out the bucket and hung it on the wall. "I'm glad to have ya help, Nate. You're a good worker. I'm slowing down a bit these days, and it's good to have a young man to do some of the grunt work."

"I was born and raised on a farm out on the prairies. I'm not afraid of hard work; Pa always worked us boys hard."

"And I'm happy to hire a friend of Ben Simmons. We've known 'im from the church for many years. If he vouches for ya, that's good enough for me. I'm just sorry I can't pay ya more, Lad. Ya work hard, but we're just a small livery, and we do okay, but I can't give ya more'n twenty-five cents a week."

Nate smiled, and reached for the oil bottle, lifted a rag to the lid, tipped it up, and used the oil on the rag to rub into the new saddle. "I'm grateful for whatever you can give me. It just feels good to be able to work and to put some by and give to the church."

Mr. Long led Jim, the large Clydesdale, out of the first stall. He got the horse to put one large foot up on the stump and went to work on his hoof with a file. "What ya saving for?"

"I wanna go home, Sir."

"Back to the prairies?"

"Robertson Township, Minnesota." Nate's grin grew wide.

"What do you plan to do?" George lifted the large hoof onto his bent knee and reached into his pocket for his hoof pick.

Nate hung the saddle over the rail and reached for the next one and the oil bottle again. "I'm not sure yet. I can't go back to law school here. A former boss has made sure I'll never be allowed back." He sighed. "I'm not sure what the Lord has in store for me, but I'm feeling drawn back home. If I can get passage back home, I'll work with my pa and Mic on the farm for a time or get a job in town and spend the time petitioning the Lord for His will." *These words sound so normal to me now; I can't believe I didn't turn to the Lord sooner! Here you are, working in a livery, living modestly, reliant on others, and you've never been more content. Well, almost...*

"You got a sweetheart?" Mr. Long moved to the front feet of the Clydesdale.

Nate placed the oil bottle down louder than he meant to and sighed.

The older man put down the horse's large foot and stood up to look at Nate. "Girl trouble, Lad?" He grimaced.

"No, it's not like that. I don't have a sweetheart. There is this incredible girl from back home. I loved her; I still love her. But I've lost my chance with her because of my own stubbornness." He shrugged.

"How so?"

"She wouldn't court because I wasn't a believer. I understand completely now, and she was absolutely right. But I'm too late." He hung his head. "I'm sure she's married by now. She had a beau last time I saw her."

"Are you sure, Son? You can't get a second chance with her?"

Nate sighed and shrugged again, hanging the last saddle on the rail. "I don't know. It's up to the Lord. I'm trying to give it over to Him to help me let go of my feelings, but no matter how much I try, I can't fall out of love with her. I guess it'll take time. For now, I'm working on getting to know the Lord, and He'll work on me in time."

"Well, I'll pray for ya, Lad. It sounds like you've got a lot of things going on right now."

Nate opened the pen of the first stall and led out a small white pony. He reached for the curry comb and went to work on her coat. "It's funny. I have no idea what the future holds; I have no home, apart from the Simmons; I have nothing to my name, this isn't even my own clothing. Yet I feel more secure about my future than I ever have before. I've been a believer nigh on three months now, and I feel free, like even though I have this uncertainty at the moment, I'm confident it's gonna work out if I just trust the Lord and be faithful to Him."

"It will, Son." The man smiled. "The one thing in this world you can count on is that God will work things together for good for those who love Him. Even the hard times happen for a reason, to teach us something, to help us grow. We don't always know the reason, but we can trust that God will see us through."

Nate grinned. "Absolutely, I understand that now and I have no doubt that He will do just that." *And I understand why Bess is the way she is now. She draws her strength from the Lord.*

∗   ∗   ∗   ∗

"You're really showing now." Bess nodded to Cass as they sat to tea at the cottage.

Cass grinned and placed one hand on her abdomen. "Yes, three months to go. Aaron is so excited."

"I know. He was fair skipping yesterday when he dropped Maisy off at the estate."

"He's a wonderful man." Cass grinned. "I've never met a stronger one. It saddens me to think of all the hurt and shame he carried for so long." Cass sipped at her chamomile tea and turned her eyes to the children playing with toy horses on the rug.

Bess nodded. "I'm so grateful to the Lord for bringing you into Aaron's life right when he needed you most. Although I'm sad about the tragedy that made it happen."

"Bess, God works all things together for good, remember? Yes, Henry's death was tragic, and I wish that hadn't happened either. But it did, and through it, God brought about amazing things."

"You're right." Bess lowered her eyes and sighed softly.

Cass squinted at her. "Bess?"

Bess raised her eyes to look at Cass, just a hint of the shine of tears in them. "I'm trying not to be ungrateful, and I'm so delighted for you all..." She sighed.

"But you're wondering when God will work it out for you too?"

"Yeah, I pray non-stop. I don't know what my future holds, where I'm supposed to be." She shrugged. "I'm starting to feel like it's time to move on. I enjoy the estate, but it isn't my future. That's one thing I am sure of. I think, maybe, it's time to go home."

Cass gave her a sad smile. "You'll work it out. We'll pray the Lord will lead you. We really will miss you though."

"Hey, it's only temporary; you'll be back after another year. I'll have your home and clinic ready for you."

"Oh, Bess, you do so much for so many people. I'm sure God will bless that and show you the way. You deserve to be happy, too."

"I am happy." She shrugged.

Cass raised her brows. "That didn't sound very convincing."

Bess chuckled and stood to refill their tea cups. "Okay, I'm content in the Lord and where He has me right now. But I feel like this season is coming to an end. But despite my uncertainties, I'm secure in the knowledge that God has me in His hands. He'll work it out."

Cass nodded. "Oh, you didn't tell me about Amber. How is her pregnancy progressing?"

Bess smiled as she sat down again and recalled the latest letter. "She's struggling a bit. She's much larger than she ought to be. She may have miscalculated the dates. Her husband works hard and isn't around a lot at the moment, and they live so far out of town. I'm trying to convince her she should move into town, or maybe get some help?"

"Like live-in help?"

"Yeah, for a time. Vincent and his father are planning a trip. Vincent's sister, Mary-Allen's husband, is terminally ill in Virginia. It's bad timing, but they have little choice."

"Oh, that's awful."

"Yeah, they hope to go and be with her, and then bring her back to Roberston Township with her small son. She has no way to make ends meet over there. Her husband was in the Navy and away a lot, but at least she had his salary to keep her going. But he's expected to pass soon, and, she wrote and told them she wants to come home."

"Oh, what a tragic story. It always saddens me to hear of people's losses. It seems like there isn't a living soul who hasn't been touched by tragedy."

"Nate is the only person I know, who's not lost anyone close to him."

"How are you feeling about that?"

"Nate?" Bess shrugged. "Resigned, I guess. I once hoped he'd be my happily ever after, but I guess God has other plans for me. I sure wish He'd show me what they are."

Cass squinted. "Maybe He has?"

"What do you mean?"

"You hope to go home soon; you say Amber'll need some help for a few weeks when her husband is away. Perhaps God is nudging you to help."

Bess's jaw fell open. "You know what? I think you might be right." Her eyes lit up. "My heart will always be drawn to Robertson Township."

Cass leaned across the table and squeezed her arm. "Pray about it, Bess. We'll pray too. God will show you."

*   *   *   *

"It feels good to wear my own clothing, and not have to borrow yours." Nate chuckled as he came downstairs in his brand-new trousers and flannel shirt; the shiny clips of the new suspenders sparkled in the lamplight.

"You look good, Lad." Angie smiled. "Can I get ya some coffee?"

"Thank you, Mrs. Simmons."

"Take a seat, Nate. Levi will be home soon."

"Looks like your savings took a hit?" Ben looked up from behind his newspaper and grimaced.

Nate sat down and reached for the cup from Mrs. Simmons's outstretched hand. He nodded his thanks to her.

"Yeah, but it was worth it. Can't go home in borrowed clothing."

"You still mean to go then?"

Nate nodded. "I'm sure God is leading me home. Two more weeks, and I'll have enough for the fare, give or take a week or so."

"You've been working hard, and I'm proud of ya. We'll really miss you, Lad." Ben's voice trembled.

"And I, you."

The door opened and Levi walked in, paper in his hands and a bemused look on his face.

"Evening." He greeted everyone, yanked on the stiff collar at his neck, and tugged it out of his black shirt. He thrust it over the hook. "Those are not comfortable." He chuckled.

"Perhaps it's too tight. I'll see what I can do for ya; loosen it up some." Angie came across to embrace her eldest. They were never shy of showing each other affection. Nate had come to admire it.

"Thanks, Ma, I'd appreciate it." He wrapped the small woman in his arms and kissed her head.

"What's put that look on your face?" Ben put down his newspaper.

Levi chuckled and took the seat next to Nate, loosened his top two buttons, and reached for the cup his mother held out to him. "Well, you know I've been praying about where the Lord wants me, and I was sure He was calling me west."

"Yes, Son, we've all been prayin' He'd guide ya."

"I went by the seminary college today. I took a class with the first years, and then the senior pastor called me aside and showed me three towns that are asking for pastors."

"That's good news, Levi. Are they in the West like you hoped?" Nate slurped at his coffee. All eyes swung anxiously to Levi to hear the news.

146

"Yeah, all three of them are, but that's not why I'm amused." He turned to Nate. "What did you say the name of your town is?"

"Robertson Township, why is one of them nearby?"

Levi grinned. "Very nearby, Robertson Township is asking for a pastor." He lifted the piece of paper. "Sounds like the old pastor is too old to manage the job now, and they want someone young there."

Nate's eyes lit up. "Oh, do come! The township could use a dedicated young pastor like you. We can travel together. It would be good to have a friend, and to continue our studies together."

Levi's face lit up. "There is nothing I'd like more. As soon as I saw it, I knew that this was why the Lord brought me across your path that night, so He could use me to lead you to the Lord, and you to lead me to Robertson Township. Course, I'll have to pray on it some, make sure I'm certain it's where the Lord wants me."

"I'll pray too. But it does sound like something God would do. You always say there are no coincidences with the Lord." Nate grinned. *It sounds like God to work things out like this.*

* * * *

"You're leaving me?" Fred put his cup down and pouted dramatically, as a small child might.

Bess chuckled. "You always knew I was only here temporarily."

147

Fred sighed. "I know, but I'd got quite accustomed to you being here." He looked around. "This place will be awful lonesome on my own."

"Well, you'll have to step up the search for the new Mrs. Bennet, won't you?"

Fred rolled his eyes. "It isn't going too well. I just don't feel anything for these women. Most are spoiled and snobbish. I've had a few fathers eye me up for their daughters, but I can't abide arranged marriages. They aren't all bad, I know that, but it isn't for me. I trust the Lord will bring the right woman at the right time."

"I'll be praying for you."

"And I, you, Bess. Oh, I'm gonna miss you more than you know, but I'll be praying the Lord guides you. He'll show you where He wants you in time. Perhaps He's got a chap waiting back there that you'll fall head over heels in love with and forget all about Nate."

Bess grimaced. "Perhaps, but like you, I won't try to make it happen. I trust the Lord."

"When will you go?"

"I'm thinking three weeks. Amber's brother-in-law is still holding on at this stage, but Vincent and his father will leave on the first of May anyway. I want to be there a few days before they leave just to settle in and make sure Amber isn't alone. She'll be close to her due date by then. She's virtually housebound now. Oh, I wish I could go to her sooner, but I have so many things to wrap up here."

"The Lord will be with her, and you'll be there before the men leave."

"Yes. I'm sorry to miss Aaron's baby, but Amber needs me for now, and I know the Lord is leading me back home."

"What will you do after the baby is born?"

"I'm not sure yet. I have time to work it out. I guess I'll move into the little apartment, and get a job at the dress shop again. The Lord will show me. In the meantime, as much as I've enjoyed being here, I can't wait to go home."

"They say home is where the heart is, and if your heart is there, I guess no other place will really ever feel like home."

"You're very wise, Cousin. I hope you'll come and visit sometime."

"I'll do my best; it's a little primitive for me." He grimaced.

"If I could adjust to this, you can adjust to that, besides it need only be for a short time."

"We'll write anyway, and see where the Lord leads."

"Amen. Isn't it wonderful not having to worry about what the future holds? Even when it's uncertain, the Lord has it all planned."

Fred nodded and lifted the coffee cup to his lips.

Fifteen

"Breathe in that good Minnesota air," Nate teased.

Levi chuckled and put his face to the open window of the stage. "It smells good, my friend."

"Five miles from Robertson Township. I can't wait to see the place again."

"How long since you've been home?"

"Two years, and I couldn't wait to get out of there. Bess had just refused me...."

Levi nodded and changed the subject. "I can't believe they have a brand-new pastorage ready for me. I'm glad you've decided to live with me. I'd hate to live alone."

"Yeah, Pa got me a job at the livery. It's not forever, but at least for over the summer while I work out what God wants. It's a good job."

"Didn't he need help on the farm?"

"I forgot to tell you. Micah got married last month. He's only just nineteen, and his bride is seventeen. They are moving into the farmhouse. Micah and Pa can manage the farm, so he asked around, and Mr. Jenkins needs help at the livery for a time. The young man he had working for him, headed West. It doesn't pay much, but I'm grateful for what I can get, and the Lord will provide."

Levi nodded. "Amen. God works all things out."

"He sure does." Nate nodded.

They sat in silence for a time. They'd had the stage to themselves since Liberty City.

"Say, Levi."

"Yeah."

Nate turned and leaned back against the wall. "I've been thinking and praying."

"'Bout what?"

"Baptism."

Levi grinned. "You wanna get baptized?"

"I do. I'm serious about serving the Lord. I'm sorry I didn't do it sooner. Bess tried to tell me, but I'm thankful to her and the seeds she planted. But no matter what happens in my life, I want to serve the Lord."

Levi slapped his back. "I'd be honored to baptize you, my friend."

"Well, let's get settled, and in a few weeks, we'll do it."

Levi grinned, and Nate's eyes sparkled as they pulled to a halt in Robertson Township. His face lit up. "Home sweet home."

Levi chuckled.

*   *   *   *

"Good Sermon, Pastor Simmons." Connie shook his hand.

"Thank you, Miss?" Levi raised his brows.

"Arnold, Connie Arnold." He nodded to her and took her hand, and turned his eyes to the woman next to her. "This is my younger sister Tam." Connie gripped her sister's arm.

Levi took her hand and looked into her eyes. "Miss Arnold." He felt his heart rate speed up just slightly as he took in her delicate features and soft brown eyes.

"Thank you for your sermon, Pastor Simmons. We're glad you're here. I trust you've settled in well?"

"Yes, thank you, Ma'am." He couldn't take his eyes from hers. "The pastorage is very comfortable. I'm enjoying living with Nate." He nodded to his approaching friend.

"Yeah, you could do worse in a housemate than me, although neither of us can cook much." Nate shook Levi's hand. "Good sermon, Pastor."

"Thank you."

Tam turned to look at Nate. "Never thought I'd see you in a church. It's almost as surprising as seeing Aaron Carter here."

Nate shrugged. "What can I say? The Lord captured me."

"I'm glad, Nate." Tam gripped his arm briefly. "Good to have you home."

"Yeah, I've been so busy. I work and sleep; that's about it."

"I hope you'll come to the dance in two weeks?" Tam asked as they walked down the stairs.

Nate shrugged. "I dunno, I'll go if Levi does. Perhaps you know a lovely girl who could take the pastor to the dance?" He gave her a knowing grin.

Tam bit her lip and blushed.

"What are you suggesting, Mr. Sawyer?" Connie squinted at him.

"Didn't you see the way the pastor's eyes lit up when he saw Tam? Had his eyes on you at the café last night too, but didn't have the courage to ask your name."

Tam blushed again. "He's right handsome."

"'Bout time you fell for a good guy." Connie chuckled.

Tam swatted at her sister. "Connie. I never said I'd fallen for him." Her cheeks colored despite the sincerity of her words.

"Tell ya what." Nate grinned. "Connie, I'll take you to the dance; if you go with the pastor, Tam. I can tell him it's a favor to me?"

Connie raised her brows. "Been home less than a week and already matchmaking, Sawyer?"

Nate chuckled. "No, only God can make a match, but there's no harm in spending time with someone, and seeing where the Lord leads."

"What about you? I know you aren't interested in me. I'm so much older than you, for starters."

"You're a nice woman, Connie, and I like you a lot. It's just, well, it's complicated."

"It's okay. I agree to your plan. It'll be fun."

"Alright, agreed. I'll be so busy between now and then, I might not see you until that evening. I'm learning the run of the livery. Mr. Jenkins will be away for a few weeks soon, and he's leaving me on my own." He grimaced.

"That's okay. What say we come to your place at, say, seven o'clock? Save you having to collect us. You live right next door to the church."

"That sounds good. I look forward to it. And Tam, you leave the pastor to me." Nate patted both women on the shoulder and hurried up the stairs into the pastorage.

153

Tam and Connie farewelled him and strolled toward town. "I can't believe the change in Nathaniel Sawyer." Tam shook her head.

"I know. He was always nice enough, but he never had the slightest interest in God."

"It's a shame?"

"A shame?"

"He and Bess Carter would have been so good together."

Connie shrugged as they pushed open the door to the café. "Well, we can't force these things to happen. At least through it all, he's come to a saving faith in Christ."

"That is good news. First Aaron and now Nate. It's good to see how God changes lives."

"And Nate's getting baptized the day after the dance."

"I know. It's wonderful."

"I agree. It's such good news." Tam walked through into the large kitchen and put the coffee pot on.

*   *   *   *

"Thank you for the ride, Mr. Clarke. Sorry you had to fetch me so late in the evening."

"My pleasure, Bess. I was in Liberty anyway, collecting these supplies to deliver. It's been nice to have your company for a few hours. Amber will be most grateful to have you here."

He leaped off to help her down. Bess's luggage would follow in a few weeks; the freight was backed up in

Chicago. He lifted down her small case and bag and walked her into the house.

"Bess." Amber painfully pushed herself up from the couch and waddled over to embrace her friend.

"Amber. Oh, look at you." Bess pulled back, and with her hands on Amber's arms, she looked her up and down. "You are absolutely glowing."

"And so uncomfortable. I'm glad you're here. I'm going to be so lonesome without Vincent.

Hearing voices, Vincent hurried into the room. He shook Mr. Clarke's hand and embraced Bess. "Thank you for coming, Bess. I feel so much better about going with you here."

"I'm sorry to come so late at night. My train was delayed. I'm glad your pa was willing to wait for me, despite the hour."

"It's my pleasure, Bess. But I must go. My life doesn't stop, I'm afraid. I have to go to Trappers Rest tomorrow, deliver this gear." He gestured to the telegraph equipment on the back of his wagon.

"Coop's doing fine in your absence, Sir." Vincent nodded.

"How do you know?" Amber laughed. "You barely leave the farm."

Vince chuckled. "You're right. It's been a while. I'm almost a hermit these days."

"Like Aaron was." Amber rolled her eyes.

Bess shook her head. *Same old Amber!*

* * * *

155

"You look lovely, Miss Archer." Nate grinned.

"Thank you, kind sir." Connie bowed.

Tam and Levi looked at each other shyly. Levi swallowed and handed her a single flower. "You look lovely too." His shining eyes confirmed it.

"Thank you." Tam's cheeks colored.

Connie and Nate looked at each other and grinned as they observed the pair. "Come on you two. You can make eyes at each other later. Now we have a dance to get to," Nate teased.

Levi and Tam blushed. They looked at each other and laughed nervously.

"You're getting a little ahead of yourselves." Tam chuckled.

"I'd say." Levi frowned at Nate. "Let's just see where God leads." He winked at Tam, a sudden peace washing over him. The Lord would guide if it was meant to be. He put his arm out to her. "Shall we?"

"Thank you, Pastor."

The four hurried out the door.

* * * *

"Bess, you should go to the dance."

"I can't leave you, Amber. You can barely move."

"I'll stay with her," Amber's mother-in-law offered.

"Go on, Bess. You've been cooped up here with me for two weeks. You haven't even been to town once. You didn't even make it to church." Amber chuckled.

"You had those false labor pains. I wasn't going to leave you."

"I appreciate all you've done for me, but you can't be a hermit just because I am. Everyone would love to see you. They don't even know you're here. Tam and Connie will be so shocked. They ask about you all the time. We've all missed you so."

"Are you sure?" Bess raised her brows.

"I'm sure. You didn't put on that beautiful gown just for me. Now go. Have a good time."

"Okay, but I won't stay late." She bent down to kiss Amber on the cheek. "Thank you, Mrs. Alexander."

"It's my pleasure, Bess. You go and have a good time."

"I'll drive you." Coop walked in with an armful of firewood. "I'm going anyway. I just came to do the firewood." He grinned at his sister.

"That's kind, Coop, and thank you for doing the wood. I never was much good with the axe; it's my weak hand." Bess chuckled.

"It's my pleasure. Maybe you'll let me accompany you. Just as a friend."

"Thank you, Coop. I'd like that." Bess grinned at him.

"Very well, I'll bring her back safe and sound, I promise." He smiled to his sister and Mrs. Alexander.

Amber rubbed her stomach and grinned. "Have fun, kids. Don't stay out too late."

Bess chuckled. "Yes, Ma." She winked and followed Coop out the door.

* * * *

Tam and Connie stood behind the beverage stand. They had been dancing with the men for a time, but they needed to multitask.

The men stood in the opposite corner with their coffee cups. "So, how's it going with Tam?" Nate gestured to the women.

Levi's cheeks colored. "Never felt this way about a girl I've just met before. It's somewhat overwhelming."

"Well, good for you, Pastor." Nate gripped his shoulder. "I'll be pray... What on earth?"

Levi frowned as Nate's eyes bulged and his face lit up. He turned to look where Nate's gaze was focused. He noticed the lovely dark-haired woman walk in with the young telegraph operator. She wore a beautiful soft pink gown and ivory gloves.

Nate swallowed twice and gasped. "Bess," he said under his breath. A wide, slow smile crossed his face.

Levi's eyes grew wide. "That's Bess?"

"What's she doing here?" Nate shook his head, momentarily paralyzed to the spot.

She greeted old friends at the door. Connie and Tam shrieked and ran headlong through the crowd to embrace her. Nate stepped out from behind Levi and walked towards her.

Bess noticed the movement and caught his eye. She gasped, gulped, and bit her lip. Tears immediately flooded her eyes, and she looked like she'd seen a ghost. Tam and Connie frowned and turned to see Nate standing behind them.

"No." Bess turned and flew out the door as fast as she was able. She ran around the corner of the building and leaned against the wall. Her chest heaving and her heart racing. Tears streamed down her face. "What is he doing here? Lord, did you bring us to the same town to torture us? I can't do this again."

"I'll go to her," Connie offered.

Nate put a hand on her arm and stopped her. "No, please, allow me?"

Connie and Tam nodded. They looked at Levi and shrugged, then turned back to the dance.

Nate hurried out, into the twilight. He found Bess around the side of the church, hands over her face sobbing. Instinctively he reached for her and pulled her into an embrace.

She didn't resist him and wept against his chest. Finally, she stepped back. "Nate, what are you doing here?"

"I might ask you the same thing?"

"I thought you were in Chicago, at law school."

He shrugged. "Life had other plans for me, I guess. I've moved home, for good." He grinned that slow, easy grin that made her heart race.

Bess closed her eyes. *No, Lord, this is too much to bear. I can't go through this again.*

But God was silent.

Bess dropped her head.

"Why are you here?" Nate's body was on fire. All those carefully pushed-down feelings were resurfacing. He felt like he was going to explode.

Bess wouldn't look at him. She couldn't. Her lips trembled, and gentle tears fell. "I've been here for two weeks, looking after Amber out at our old farm. She's close to her due date, and her husband is in Virginia." Her voice was quiet and full of emotion.

"I haven't seen you in town? I've been here nearly a month."

"I haven't been to town at all. Her brother has been delivering us groceries, and she's been struggling a lot, so I never even got to church." *Oh Lord, I've never known agony like this. Please, I beg of You, take these feelings from me. I can't allow myself to love him.*

"I wonder why Coop didn't tell us. I was in the post office a few days ago."

"He probably just didn't think to." She was trying hard to make conversation casually, all the while screaming inside. "Besides I had told him I wanted to surprise my friends at the dance and just appear, like Cinderella or something." She lifted her blue eyes to him. "How foolish." She hung her head again. The love in his eyes was too much to bear.

"Not foolish at all. When I saw you, I thought I was looking at an angel. My knees nearly buckled. You're so beautiful, Bess." He cupped her chin and lifted her face to look at him.

Her lips trembled, and her eyes filled with tears. "Oh, I can't do this again." She pulled away from him, lifted her skirts, and hurried towards the farm.

"Bess," he called after her.

"No," she said loudly without stopping. "I can't."

"Oh, Bess." He hung his head. "Lord, give me strength to know how to handle this. I can't bear to see her hurting."

Connie came out to look for them. She heard Bess call out and watched her run away. "What happened?"

"I'm sure she just got a fright at seeing me again. I'm afraid we didn't part well in Chicago."

Connie put a hand to her mouth and the other on his arm. "Nate, I'm sorry."

"It's okay. I'll go and see her tomorrow, after my baptism, when the shock has worn off."

The pain in his eyes and the furrow to his brow made her ask, "You still love her, don't you?"

Nate gave her a sad smile. "With my whole heart. I will 'till my dying day."

Connie sighed. "I hope it works out for you both."

Nate shrugged. "I'm not so sure. I believe she has a beau back in the city."

"Ohhh. I didn't know that. Why is she back? Did she say?"

"Amber is housebound now and struggling. With her husband away, Bess came back to be with her for the duration. She's been here two weeks."

"Two weeks?" Connie's eyebrows flew up. "And nobody knew?"

Nate shrugged. "The farm is out of town, and only Coop knew."

"That boy always has his head in the clouds. He wouldn't think to tell anyone if the entire town was on fire. Come on, let's go back to the dance, Bess needs time to calm down."

Nate looked sadly into the distance, sighed, and nodded. He turned to walk back to the dance, but his heart wasn't in it. He left early and headed for his room to pray.

*   *   *   *

"Bess?" Amber turned when Bess came flying in, in tears.

"Oh." Bess gulped and ran to her room.

"Bess," Amber called to the pink blur that streaked past her.

Mrs. Alexander came out of the kitchen. "What's happened?"

"I don't know. She just came in crying. Please help me up so I can go to her?"

"Sure."

Amber waddled down the hallway clinging to the wall.

"Bess." She knocked on the door and paused for a moment to listen. She pushed it open and walked in. Her friend was sobbing on the bed. Amber sat next to her and stroked her hair as Bess lay face down.

"Bess, what on earth has happened?"

Bess sat up and sniffed loudly. Amber had never seen such agony on her face. "Oh, Bess, what is it? Tell me."

Bess's lips trembled and she lifted the handkerchief to her eyes. She took a deep breath and sniffed again. "Nate."

"Nate? What about Nate?"

"He's in town. He was at the dance."

"Ohhhh, Bess. Did he say something?"

"No. He was very kind. It just caught me off guard, I didn't know he was here. I wasn't expecting to see him. It's brought up all the feelings again."

Amber squeezed her arm. "Oh, I'm sorry. Coop didn't tell me he was here, or I would have warned you."

"Coop is airy sometimes. He doesn't pay much attention." Bess sniffed again.

"So what does this mean?"

"I don't know. But I can't do this again. Getting over Nate has been the hardest thing in my life."

Amber raised her brows. "You're not over him, are you?"

Bess closed her eyes and a sob escaped her. "No. I love him. I always have."

"Bess, I can't bear to see you hurting. Can't you just accept him?"

"I can't, Amber. I can't. I won't be with an unbeliever. I've told you that."

"But you're in pain?"

"I know. I have to find a way to fall out of love with him. I can't be in the same town as him."

Amber frowned. "What are you saying?"

"I don't know. I need to pray, I guess. I need God to help me with this. I can't go through all this again."

Amber put her arm around Bess and kissed her hair. "I can't imagine what it's like to love someone as much as you love Nate and not be able to be with them. Especially when he loves you so deeply too."

"I don't know if he does anymore. I think he might. He told me I was beautiful." Bess sniffed and smiled. "I'll be okay. I just want some time to pray. I can't wait to go to church tomorrow. At least I know Nate won't be there!" She sighed.

"Mrs. Alexander told me the service is at The Island tomorrow. Evidently, there's a new young pastor in town, and he's taking a baptismal service."

"That's just what I need. Some happy news, and The Island is my favorite spot. It's a shame it reminds me so much of Nate. But I'll be okay. The Lord will help me. Sorry you had to come in here when you are so uncomfortable."

"That's okay. You're my best friend. I'm not going to sit by while you are hurting."

Sixteen

Bess was running late for the service. Amber had been feeling unwell, Mrs. Alexander arrived a little after the time Bess needed to leave. Oh, how she needed to commune with the Lord, to have Him minister to her broken heart. The joy of a baptism would be wonderful and she looked forward to meeting the new young pastor. Mrs. Alexander didn't know much about him, it wasn't often she attended church.

Bess pulled up the gig and leaped down, tethered it, and hurried through the glade. "Lord, please help me. Show me what it is you want for me. Help me with this agonizing burning love in my heart. I can't bear it. I need you to take it from me." She determinedly sniffed back the tears as she reached The Island.

She couldn't see over the top of the gathered congregation but could hear the pastor talking from the water.

"On your confession of faith, here before these witnesses, I baptize you in the name of the Father, The Son, and the Holy Spirit." Levi dunked his friend under the water and pulled him up again.

Nate grinned as a peace swept over him. *I Am with you. I have you in My hand,* a voice deep in his soul whispered. Nate nodded. He trusted God with everything, even with Bess. He was sad she wasn't there, but he understood why and he'd find her later and talk to her. He embraced Levi, and the men walked out of the water. As they did, the crowd parted, and Bess looked up to see Nate and Levi walking out of the water,

165

arms around each other's shoulders. Her hand flew to her mouth, and she gasped. "Nate?" Her heart lurched and she let out a single sob. Everyone turned in time to see her run away again.

She hurried over the bridge and stopped in the glade. Falling onto one of the wooden chairs, she buried her head in her hands and sobbed.

Nate looked up to see her run away. "Bess." He snatched the towel from Connie's hands. "Thanks for coming." He ran to find Bess.

"Bess." He fell into the seat beside her, with the towel wrapped around his shoulders. He pulled her into his arms and let her cry. He leaned his head against hers and stroked her hair. "Oh, Bess, I can't bear to see you hurting."

At last, she stopped crying and stood up from the chair. Her eyes were full of hurt, and love, and confusion. "You..." She stopped. There were no words. She dropped her head and exhaled loudly.

Nate stood up and lifted her chin so he could look into her eyes. "Bess, I wanted to tell you last night, but you ran away before I could."

"You got baptized?" Her eyes sparkled as a glimmer of hope rose in her.

There was that smile again, the one that nearly made her knees collapse. She gasped at the overwhelming feelings that washed over her.

"Yes, Levi – the new pastor - is my friend. I lived with his family for a time. It's a long story, but they showed me real Christian love, and I realized what a wretched fool I was and that you were right all along. I gave my heart to Christ on Christmas Day." He couldn't help but smile, and the way his eyes shone was evidence enough that he meant it.

Bess closed her eyes and tears streamed down her cheeks. "Nate. Oh, Nate." She still had no words.

He turned his back and walked away two steps. He took a deep breath as his heart lurched. To know that he had no chance with her after all that had happened was agonizing. He took a deep breath and turned back to look at her. "I know I'm too late, Bess, and I'm so sorry I hurt you all this time. But I do hope you are happy?"

"Happy?" She looked up at him.

"With your beau."

"I don't have a beau."

"Well, your husband then. Whoever he is. I hope he makes you happy."

"Nate. I don't have a beau or a husband." She shrugged. "Or anyone."

Nate's heart flipped so hard he nearly collapsed. He took two steps just so he could hold onto the chair. He took a deep breath and tears stung his eyes.

"Bess. All this time, I thought you were married and living in Chicago, and my heart has been broken, and trampled on. I've never stopped loving you, not even for a second. I know how much my stubbornness and unwillingness to listen has hurt you and I beg for your forgiveness." He took two steps away, then turned to face her. She had her hands over her face and was weeping. Nate closed his eyes. "I know I don't deserve your forgiveness, and you've no doubt moved on. My hopes at a second chance are slim.

"I've done everything I can to try to get you out of my heart, but the more I tried, the deeper I fell in love with you." He swiped at his tears. "I can't bear to see you hurt. I promise you, I'll leave town tomorrow, so you won't ever have to see me again." He finished with a loud sob and trembling lips.

Bess said nothing. Her hands remained over her face, and her body shook with heart-wrenching sobs.

Nate sniffed away his tears and nodded twice. His face curled up in pain. "Goodbye, Bess. I'll never love another as I love you." He turned and walked away, sucking in deep breaths.

Bess lifted her head. "Nate," she called.

He stopped walking, closed his eyes, and took a deep breath.

"Nate, please don't go," she cried out through her tears.

His heart lurched again. *Trust me, I know the plans I have for you.* A voice sang from deep in his soul. He grinned and turned around.

Bess smiled, exhaled loudly and ran to him. "Nate." She threw her arms around him and sobbed against his wet shirt. He held her tightly again, laying his head on hers, hope building in his heart. She pulled back from him and looked up into his dark eyes. "All I ever wanted was to hear that you've given your heart to the Lord. I never imagined it was possible." Joy and hope shone from her eyes.

Nate tenderly stroked a tear from her cheek. She trembled and fixed soft blue eyes on him. "Please don't go," she pleaded. "I love you, too. I've never stopped loving you. I've been in pain for so long, because all I ever wanted was to throw myself in your arms and tell you how much I have always loved you."

"Bess." He cupped her cheek and his deep brown eyes searched her face. "Is there any chance you could forgive me?" A tear streaked down his cheek. "Is there any way you'd give me a second chance?"

"Yes, of course, Nate."

"Ohhhhh." He leaned his head back as a surge of joy swept through his heart. Breathing deeply, blissful tears ran from his eyes.

A peace washed over him, and he felt God prompting him. "Bess. I have no money, and half a law degree. My life has been such a mess until I found the Lord. I understand now why you refused me, and you were right to do so. But now, by some miracle." He sniffed back a tear. "The Lord has reunited us. He's given me a second chance, and I'm hoping, oh, I'm praying that you'll give me a second chance too."

Bess bit her lip. She couldn't keep the tears from falling.

Nate flashed her that grin, prayed for courage, and kissed the hand he held. With God's prompting in his heart, he dropped to his knee. "Bess Carter, I don't have a ring. I don't know what the future holds. But I love you with all my heart, and I don't ever want to be without you again."

Bess gasped. "Oh, Nate." Her voice trembled. Her heart was dancing, and she was on the brink of collapsing.

"Bess, you are my heart's safe haven. I need you by my side. Will you marry me?"

Bess burst into tears as the overwhelming emotions engulfed her. She put her spare hand to her face. Nate frowned, hoping he hadn't blown it. She took a deep breath, opened her eyes and smiled. "Of course." Her lips trembled.

Nate's face lit up. "You will?" He jumped up and wrapped her in his arms, lifting her off her feet. "Oh, Bess, this is the best day of my life for two reasons my baptism and you in my arms."

"Nate, this is all I ever prayed for."

Nate put her down and brushed at her cheek tenderly with his knuckles. His eyes fixed on hers, the love in them overwhelmed her.

"I'm sorry, I've made you all wet." He raised his brows.

"I don't care. I wouldn't care if you were covered in mud. I just want to be in your arms, at last." She sighed loudly.

He pulled her close again and spoke into her hair, "Thank you for giving me a second chance. Now that I have your heart, I will cherish it till my dying day."

"I know. Me too." Her voice was soft and dreamy.

He squeezed her and then pulled back from her to look her in the eyes. Flashing her the smile that made her knees week, he let his eyes talk to hers.

He leaned in slowly and brought his lips to hers. Bess closed her eyes, and slipped her arms around his neck. Her knees buckled, but he held her tightly as their hearts sang to each other in that kiss.

To be able to kiss her, knowing she was his at last, made his entire body light up with electricity. He pulled back from her, and cupped her cheek again, keeping his eyes fixed on hers. "I love you."

"Oh, Nate. I can't believe I can finally let myself love you." She sobbed. She smiled at him and then lay her head against his wet shirt. "This is the only place I ever wanted to be."

"It's the only place I ever want you to be." He kissed her hair. "Thank the Lord for second chances."

She nodded against his chest, joy radiated through her heart. Finally she was free to love Nate.

Bess shrugged. "I think it's finished."

Nate wrapped his arm around her waist and looked around at the little apartment. "Our little love nest. I can't wait to move in here with you in a few days' time."

"Four days, Nate. I can't believe it. Thank you for all your help to get it set up, and ready for our use."

"My pleasure. It's our home after all. At least to begin with."

"For two months or so."

Nate squinted. "Why only two months?"

Bess bit her lip and stepped away from him. She hurried to the kitchen to put the coffeepot on. A wry smile crossed her face and she tried hard to appear nonchalant.

Nate walked slowly up to her, put one hand on her waist and lifted her chin. "Bess, why only two months?" He raised his brows.

"I did something." She raised her shoulders and put her hands on his chest.

Nate squinted at her. "What did you do, Miss Carter?"

"Let me bring some coffee and I'll tell you." She passed Nate a plate of cookies, her damaged hand wobbled as she almost lost her grip. He took it from her quickly and placed it on the table.

He hurried back to fetch the coffee cup from her left hand before it spilled everywhere. "Allow me?"

Bess passed him both cups. "I'm sorry you have to."

"Don't be sorry. I want to help, I know your hand gets sore when you've been using it a lot." He lay the cups down and took the seat beside her on their new couch. "Now, explain yourself, M'lady."

Bess put her hand into her apron pocket and pulled out two envelopes. She passed him the top one. "Please don't be mad." Her eyes pleaded.

Nate frowned and took the envelope. "Why would I be mad?" He flicked his eyes down to the envelope with his name on it. "The University of Minneapolis?"

Bess lowered her eyes.

Nate lifted her chin. "Bess?"

"You told me you couldn't finish your law degree and that if you could you would like to. Well turns out Cousin Fred is very connected and knows people at the University in Minneapolis. So I..." She bit her lip.

Nate put the envelope down and gripped her hand. "Bess, there is absolutely nothing you can't say to me."

She nodded. "I took the liberty of applying on your behalf to the new law school and..." She gestured to the envelope. "That's the response."

Nate furrowed his brows slightly and then grinned. "You did that for me?"

"Mmhm. I hope you aren't mad, I wanted it to be a surprise. I wasn't trying to be sneaky." She hung her head again.

Nate cupped her chin and lifted her head. "I'm not mad. I love you so much. I know you did this because you love me and I'm thrilled you did." He grimaced then. "I guess I have to see if I made it in." He leaned forward and kissed her. "A kiss for courage."

Bess giggled. "Open it."

He slipped open the envelope and pulled out the sheet of paper unfolded it and read aloud,

"Dear Mr. Nathaniel Sawyer.

We are delighted to offer you a full scholarship in the law department ..."

He didn't read anymore. Bess gasped. "Oh, Nate."

He dropped the letter and threw his arms around her, pulled her close and kissed her hair. "Thank you for this. Are you sure you won't mind going to Minneapolis for a year?"

She sat back from him. "Of course not. It's only a year and we'll get back the same time as Aaron and Cass and it'll be wonderful."

"You really are something. I guess we'll have to save some money for a small apartment. I couldn't ask you to live with me in the boarding house." He grimaced. "You deserve better than that."

"Nathaniel Sawyer, I would happily live with you in the boarding house, or in a barn for that matter."

Nate closed his eyes. "I couldn't let you do that. We don't have to go. It's just a nice dream."

Bess tucked her lips under again and her cheeks reddened.

Nate squinted at her. "There's something else isn't there?"

"Mmhm." She grinned and passed him the other envelope.

"What is this?"

"Well you remember I told you I'm an heiress and I bought the clinic for Aaron and Cass?"

Nate nodded and waited for her to continue.

"Well I was so certain you were going to be accepted into the university, I did something."

"What?"

"Open it."

He nodded and slipped out a sheet of paper. It was the deed to a house. He looked at her and frowned. "You bought a house?"

She nodded. "I have a friend in Minneapolis and she found us a little apartment next door to her cousin's home. It's one street back from the university and an easy walk to the main street of town."

Nate shook his head. "You bought a house?"

"Mmmhmm. We can sell it again when we leave."

Nate ran his tongue across his teeth. "You are really something, Miss Carter. I feel so blessed. Thank you."

"You're welcome, Nate. I'm so proud of you and I want to see you live your dreams. I'll be thrilled to be there beside you the whole way."

Nate pulled her close and kissed her deeply. He lay his forehead on hers. "Thank you. I'm thrilled to have you there with me. And I am living my dream. Having you in my arms is the greatest dream I ever had. I'm just sorry I'm not providing for you."

Bess frowned. "What are you saying?"

"Bess. I don't want you to spend your money on me?"

Bess sat back and looked at him, her eyes fixed on his. "Nathaniel Sawyer, do you love me?"

"Of course."

"Do you want to marry me?"

"More than I want to breathe."

"Then there is no more, 'me' or 'my money'." She put a hand on his cheek. "There is only, 'us,' and 'our money.' And I think we should put *our* money to good use, get your law degree, it'll only be one more year and then you can sit the bar, and we'll come home and you can open a practice. You'll be a wonderful lawyer."

Nate pulled her to him and kissed her hair. He closed his eyes and let his tears fall unhindered.

"What touches you, Nate?"

"A few months ago my life nearly ended. I hit rock bottom and now, I can't believe the blessings the Lord has heaped on me."

"Yes, He does that. He doesn't promise us a life of abundance, and this may be just a season. You never know what might happen. So let's make the most of it while we can. My dreams have all come true, and I just wanna bask in it for as long as I can."

"It proves that God looks after those who honor Him. You stuck to your convictions at great personal cost. Bess, I've never known someone as strong as you."

"You have no idea how many times I nearly caved. You are so wonderful and were quite the temptation. But God is everything to me, Nate. I was prepared to live the life of spinster for Him."

"You would have found someone else."

"No, my heart has only ever been yours." She looked at him. "To love another man would be treasonous to me."

Nate grinned, that smile that melted her heart. He cupped her cheek and kissed her deeply. "I am so in love with you, Bess. Four days can't come soon enough. I don't ever want you out of my arms."

"Nate we can't be together twenty-four hours a day, even when we are married. We have to work."

"More's the pity. Can't we just do this all day instead?"

"No, we have to meet the stage remember."

"I remember." He kissed her again and she stood to take their cups to the kitchen. Nate followed her.

She turned around and Nate was kneeling before her holding out a ring box.

"Nate?"

"I'm so sorry, I haven't got you an engagement ring until now." He shrugged. "I haven't had the money."

"Oh, Nate. I don't need an engagement ring. I'll be happy to just wear a wedding band. You should have kept your money."

He grinned and took her hand. He flicked open the box.

A purple stone sparkled in the lamplight. Bess put her hand over her mouth.

"Will you marry me?"

"Nate, I already said yes to you more than three weeks ago." She chuckled.

He grinned. "Yes but it's not official until you have a ring."

She nodded. "Okay, ask me again."

"With pleasure." He took her hand and kissed it. "Elizabeth Rose Carter, will you be my wife?"

"Yes, of course I will." Bess gave him a wide smile.

Nate stood up and pulled her close, kissed her deeply then lay his head on hers. "I should ask you that every day, the thrill of having you say yes to me is best feeling I've ever experienced."

"I think hearing 'I do.' Will be even better."

He grinned. "You're right."

"May I see the ring?"

"Of course." He pulled it from the box and slipped it on a finger on her damaged hand.

"It's so beautiful. I've not seen this at the store."

"I didn't get it from the store."

She tilted her head and frowned. He gestured to the table. Bess nodded and took a seat next to him.

"It was my mothers."

"Your mother gave you her ring?" Bess frowned.

"There is something you don't know about my family?"

"Oh?"

"My pa is actually my step-father and Micah is my half-brother."

"Really? You look so much like him."

"He's also my uncle." He chuckled. "I know it sounds a little weird but my real father died before I was born. Ma was madly in love with him and they'd only been married six months. His name was Nathaniel Harrison Sawyer. They moved out here with his brother, Charlie, just after they were married. When he died, Uncle Charlie took pity on Ma and took her in, but that wouldn't have been appropriate unless they were married, so they agreed to get married, and over time they fell in love and Micah came along. "

"How come you've never told me?"

Nate shrugged. "It never occurred to me. I never knew my father, and Uncle Charlie, Pa, adopted me when I was born. He's the only pa I've ever known."

"And it explains your two middle names. Nathaniel Charles Harrison Sawyer."

"Yeah, Ma gave me the name of both my fathers. And last night I told them I was saving for a ring. Ma gasped and ran to her room. She came out and gave me this. It was the ring my father gave her. Pa, Uncle Charlie, brought her another one years later. But she kept my father's ring to give to me one day, to give to my lovely lady. But if you don't like it, I can get you another one, one you can choose." He grimaced. "I need to save a little more. I just thought you might like to have a ring on your finger so all the young men in the world know you're unavailable." He chuckled.

Bess grinned. "I never knew all of that. I'm sorry about your real pa, I know how it feels to lose family."

"I never knew him, Bess. I'm sad I never did but I don't miss him because I never knew him. Charlie has been a wonderful father to me, it was never even discussed that I wasn't his son. I just always was. And Micah and I have always been close."

"I can understand that. Aaron loves Maisy and Henry like they are his own."

"Well, anyhow, you can choose a different ring if you want to."

Bess lifted the ring up to look at it. There was a twist in the gold and a small heart-shaped purple stone sat on top. "No. I love this ring, purple is one of my favorite colors, and I'm proud to have your father's ring, it'll be like we carry a little piece of him. I wonder if you're just like him?" Bess put her hand on his cheek.

He took the hand from his cheek, and held it in both of his. "Ma says I am. I'm a bit more outgoing than Pa is and she said that Nathaniel was like that, always laughing and joking about something. She told me she fell in love with his charm, his good looks, his courage and his character."

"Yep, just like his son." Bess smiled.

Nate cupped her cheek. "Thank you, my darling. Now we should go meet the stage I guess." He lifted the hand with the ring and kissed it. Somehow on the damaged hand it was even more beautiful, a testament of her strength.

Nate gripped Bess's hand and they fell into step together in the May sunshine. "Thank you for being willing to wait a month so that Aaron and Fred could make it."

Nate winked at Bess. "Of course. I want that too. I can be patient."

"Oh, I can't wait to meet baby Mitchell."

Nate grinned. "Me either." He leaned in and whispered. "And I can't wait to have one of our own."

"Nate." Bess blushed deeply and was thankful for the distraction of the arriving stage.

* * * *

Aaron helped his sister down from the gig, careful not to snag her new pale green dress. When she was steady on her feet he turned to fetch her wildflower bouquet that Cass had prepared for her. He swiped at his eyes before turning to pass it to her.

"Aaron, are you crying?" Bess's soft blue eyes shone.

"I'm afraid so." He shrugged and gave her his arm. They walked slowly over the small arched bridge toward the clearing on The Island. "Can't help it, you are radiant, Bess. You know Pa'd be proud, of you and the man you've chosen. I am too. I'm proud of your conviction, your courage and your faith, and beyond delighted that it's all worked out for you." He kissed her hair.

"Thank you, Big Brother."

Bess stood up on her tiptoes and kissed his cheek and they paused to wait for their cue.

"Well, are you ready?" He grinned as Amber reached the front and the harpest began to play the bridal march. "This is a beautiful spot. I'm glad you chose an outdoor wedding."

Bess squeezed her brother's arm and they turned to walk over the bridge. Nate stood up with Levi, the best man and pastor.

Nate gasped in deep breaths and stretched his neck to get a glimpse of his bride as they turned towards the wide aisle between the church pews that had been carried out to The Island.

One look at Bess's beaming face and eyes full of love and Nate's tears escaped and his knees buckled. Levi chuckled and put his arm around his shoulder to hold him up.

Bess's wide smile gave Nate courage and he stood and locked eyes on hers.

If Aaron hadn't stopped before the alter, and put his hand out to halt Bess, she would have gone right on walking all the way to Nate.

Nate felt time stand still as he looked into the shining eyes of his bride. His heart threatened to explode out of his chest.

Levi gulped, and sucked back his own emotions. "Who gives this woman to be married to this man?"

Aaron, sniffed, swallowed and sniffed again. He looked at Bess. "I do."

Bess grinned at him and kissed his cheek. "I love you, Brother."

Aaron passed her hand to Nate. "Here's your bride, Nate. Cherish her."

Nate nodded and reached for her other hand. He looked her in the eye. "Hi." He gave her that smile that made her knees weak.

"Hi." She looked shyly up at him. Her cheeks a charming red and her countenance shining her love for him, making Nate's breath catch in his throat.

They said the words as Levi instructed. The pastor patted his friend on the back. "Nate. Kiss your bride."

Nate nodded and wrapped Bess in his arms. The crowd roared and whistled as the pair kissed. Nate turned his eyes to the crowd without breaking the kiss, shrugged and prolonged it, bringing laughter, more whistles and applause. Nate broke the kiss at last and brushed her cheek. "Wife," he whispered and Bess looked at him with so much love it made him gasp.

Levi wiped at his own eyes and gripped a shoulder of each. "Ladies and gentlemen, this is the most joyous announcement I could ever make. If you knew Nate six months ago, you'd know why it gives me the greatest delight..." He paused and the couple turned hand in hand to face the crowd. "To present, Mr. & Mrs. Nathaniel Sawyer."

Nate closed his eyes. He grinned and scooped Bess up in his arms. She shrieked and dropped her bouquet, throwing her arms around his neck. He kissed her again, bringing more raucous applause from the gathered crowd. "I love you, Mrs. Sawyer." He couldn't drag his eyes from her radiant face.

"I love you, Mr. Sawyer." She lay her head on his shoulder and he carried her down the aisle and finally put her on her feet at the end.

The new Mr. & Mrs. Sawyer walked hand in hand amongst their gathered friends.

The pair reached the pastor, talking to a group of young people in the corner. He turned to embrace the newlyweds.

"Thank you, Levi. I can never thank you enough for loving him." Bess stepped back, tears in her eyes.

"The only thanks I need is that look on your faces." Levi grinned. "Sure am gonna miss my housemate, it'll be awful lonely in that pastorage by myself."

Nate gripped his shoulder. "You might have to change that soon, my friend." He gestured to Tam, standing under the tree talking to Connie.

Levi's cheeks flushed and he grinned. "Can't deny it."

"She's a lovely woman, Levi. We are happy for you. I hope we get to attend another wedding soon?" Bess tipped her head to the side.

"In time." He smiled.

The newlyweds greeted Nate's parents and his brother, and they lovingly welcomed Bess to their family. Amber and Vincent embraced them and Bess kissed three week old Martha.

"I'm so excited, we are both grown up married women, Mrs. Sawyer." Amber grinned and passed the baby to her husband.

"Yes we are, Mrs. Alexander."

"I'm so thrilled." Amber lunged at Bess to wrap her in an embrace. "I'm so happy for you, Bess. I hated watching you so unhappy, loving Nate but not being able to give him your heart."

Bess squeezed her and they broke the embrace. "It was worth it in the end."

Bess turned to look at Nate and Levi. Both had knowing grins on their faces as they looked towards the pine tree. Bess followed his gaze. He was watching Fred.

"What?"

Nate put his arm around her and nodded toward Fred. "What do you make of that?"

It was then that Bess noticed the sparkle in Fred's eye. He was deep in conversation with Connie, and both sets of cheeks flushed.

Bess grinned. "Connie would make an excellent, Mrs. Bennet, lady of the manor."

"Yes, she would." Levi grinned and caught Tam's eye. He winked at her and both blushed.

Nate kissed Bess's hair. "Are you ready to go home?"

"Home." She grinned. "Our home. I can't wait. I'm tired of being alone."

"You never have to be alone again."

"Good. I'll hold you to that, Mr. Sawyer."

"I'd expect no less, Mrs. Sawyer."

"First, I need to throw my bouquet."

The single women lined up and Bess threw the flowers over her head. In mid-air it split apart and half landed in Tam's hands, and half in Connie's. The two sisters looked at each other, blushed, and then laughed hysterically.

Bess reached for her husband's hand, Nate gestured toward Levi, admiring Tam. "He's long gone, they'll be married soon, mark my words."

"I'm happy for them, Tam will make a wonderful pastor's wife, she's so caring."

Nate turned to look at Fred leaning against the tree. He couldn't hide the wide grin and nodded slowly as he watched Connie and Tam laugh over their bouquets.

"I wouldn't be surprised if your cousin sticks around for a while." Nate winked at Bess. "Well come on. I wanna take my bride home." He picked her up in his arms and kissed her.

"Are you gonna carry me all that way?"

"Of course, I'd carry you to the moon and back." He walked through their waiting friends and family stopping before her brother and his family.

"We'll meet you in the café on Wednesday at noon, before you leave." Bess smiled.

"Very well, Mr. and Mrs. Sawyer, we'll see you then. I'm so thrilled, Sis." Aaron kissed her cheek.

"I have to insist you stop kissing my bride, Sir." Nate grinned.

"Nope!" They laughed heartily and Aaron slapped his new brother-in-law on his back.

Nate nodded to the Carters and walked over the bridge. Bess lay her head on her husband's shoulder. Neither spoke until they were inside their little house and they'd shut their door.

Nate put Bess back onto her feet and cupped her cheek. "Welcome home, Mrs. Sawyer."

"Welcome home, Mr. Sawyer." Her voice was soft and dreamy.

"You ready to start our happily ever after?"

"I can't wait."

Nate kissed her deeply, and while she still had her eyes closed, he whispered in her ear. "No need to wait any more, my darling, we are living it now."

"Oh, Nate, loving you is my dream come true."

"Mine too." Nate took his bride in his arms again and kissed her again.

THE END

About the Author

Jo Dawson grew up on a dairy farm in Wellsford, a small town in the North Island of New Zealand. She spent fifteen years as a teacher in New Zealand and abroad, before becoming a stay-at-home mum and completing her graduate degree in Theology.

She has lived in Australia and the USA for a time, and these experiences have added to her love of people and history. Blessed with a vivid imagination and the love of classical literature and historical fiction, Jo virtually grew up best friends with Anne Shirley, romping with Jo March and her sisters, sailing a raft down the Mississippi with Huckleberry Finn or living in the 'little house' with Laura Ingalls.

Born and raised in a strong Christian family, Jo's faith is at the centre of who she is, with a lifetime of being involved in churches and Christian camps. These two loves, literature and the Lord, have inevitably converged into writing compelling stories of strong Christian women, courageously facing the hardships of life on the frontier. It is her hope that women of all ages would find encouragement from her heroines' experiences that, while fiction, so often mirror even our modern lives.

Jo currently resides in the small North Island town of Waipu in New Zealand, where she lives with her husband, son, father-in-law and a very lazy cat.

Other books by J. L. Dawson

Journeys of the Heart Series
Awakening of the Heart
Shepherd of the Heart
Decisions of the Heart
A Home for the Heart
Blessings of the Heart
Legacies of the Heart

Douglas Falls Series
Prequel: The Cost of Duty
A Duty to Love
Twixt Duty and Love
A Duty to Family (coming soon)

Multiple Author Series (Standalone books).

Hers to Redeem Book 14: Aaron's Anguish
Hers to Redeem Book 18: Mitchell's Misfortune
Hers to Redeem Book 21: Robbie's Roaming

Standalone Books

To Love Nate – A companion to Aaron's Anguish.

Where to find these books:
https://www.amazon.com/stores/J-L-Dawson/author
www.jodawsonauthor.com to sign up for my newsletter
jldawsonauthor@yahoo.com to write to the author
Jo Dawson on Instagram and Facebook

www.ingramcontent.com/pod-product-compliance
Lightning Source LLC
Chambersburg PA
CBHW032136170626
46808CB00006B/2254